Traitor!

His master looked anxiously at Ben's bruised face, and shook his head. "Thank heaven it wasn't worse."

But Ben's mind was on other things.

"I know you can't accuse Horsham's men of stealing, or of setting fire to the hut," he said. "But what if we found some proof? Like, how they managed to take the costumes, when Will keeps them locked in the tiring room..."

"What do you mean?" John was frowning. "You think there's a traitor in our company?"

C 03 0190159

WEST DUNBARTONSHIRE LIBRARIES	
C030190159	
HJ	05/06/2008
JF	£5.99
CL	

First published in the UK in 2008 by Usborne Publishing Ltd., Usborne House, 83-85 Saffron Hill, London EC1N 8RT, England. www.usborne.com

Copyright © John Pilkington, 2008

The right of John Pilkington to be identified as the author of this work has been asserted by him in accordance with the Copyright, Designs and Patents Act, 1988.

Cover artwork by Michael Thompson. Map by Ian McNee.

The name Usborne and the devices ♀ ⊕ are Trade Marks of Usborne Publishing Ltd.

All rights reserved. No part of this publication may be reproduced, stored in a retrieval system or transmitted in any form or by any means, electronic, mechanical, photocopying, recording or otherwise without the prior permission of the publisher.

This is a work of fiction. The characters, incidents, and dialogues are products of the author's imagination and are not to be construed as real. Any resemblance to actual events or persons, living or dead, is entirely coincidental.

A CIP catalogue record for this book is available from the British Library.

J MAMJJASOND/08 ISBN 9780746087114 Printed in Great Britain.

Shoreditch

The Old Theatre

Shoreditch Street

Finsbury Fields

The Curtain

Moorfields

The Dolphin Inn

Bishopsgate

Bishopsgate Street

Hog Lane

City Wall

Broad Street

Houndsditch

The Bull Inn

St Paul's

Thames Street

East Cheap Market

Paul's Stairs

Queenhithe

Falcon Stairs

Winchester House

The Clink

London Bridge

The Pike Garden

The Rose

Maiden Lane

St Saviour's Church

The Tower of London

The Elephant Inn

Horseshoe Lane

Southwark

Chapter One

It was all Master Shakespeare's fault. If he and his company hadn't been doing so well, Ben Button and the rest of Lord Bonner's Men would never have had to move.

Lord Bonner's players stood around on the stage of the Old Theatre in Shoreditch, by Finsbury Fields, just north of the city. Apart from the dozen or so men and boys, the big circular theatre was empty. The galleries and the stage were roofed with tiles, but the rest of the building was open to the sky. It was a sharp winter's morning, and the players' breath hung in the air like steam. Some stamped their feet to keep warm.

Ben wore his winter jerkin over his new crimson doublet. All the company had been given new clothing, in the deep red livery of their patron Lord Bonner. Their old clothes had become worn out with travelling during the summer. For Ben Button, the touring was already a memory. Now they were back in London for the winter. All had looked well when they started performing an old favourite, *The Legend of Robin Hood* – that is, until the Lord Chamberlain's Men had opened nearby at the other Shoreditch theatre, the Curtain. The Lord Chamberlain's was the most important acting company in England. Their patron was not only rich and powerful – he was the Queen's cousin. And Lord Bonner's Men had soon found themselves facing some stiff competition.

"*The Taming of the Shrew – a Comedy.*" Bonner's leading player, Hugh Cotton, was holding up a torn playbill. It advertised a new play by one of the Lord Chamberlain's men, William Shakespeare, who had come to London as an actor and was now a successful playmaker.

"It's packing them in – you can hear the laughter from Moorfields." Solomon Tree, the company's glum-faced comic, was at his gloomiest this morning.

"And what are we doing? *Robin Hood* again!"
Solomon was playing Friar Tuck, and made no secret
of the fact that he was tired of his role, as he was of
the heavy padding he wore to make himself look fat.

"We should revive another play – one with plenty
of action!" Gabriel Tucker, the company's specialist
in villain roles, spoke up quickly. The little man was
playing the Sheriff of Nottingham, and had grown a
bristly moustache which twitched whenever he was
agitated. It was twitching busily now.

Ben noticed that his master, John Symes, was
silent. Since he lodged in John's house as his prentice,
Ben knew how worried his master had been of late.
As the company's manager and one of its main
players, John had bills to settle: for costumes and
props, as well as rent for the Old Theatre, not to
mention the company's wages. And the gate receipts
for *Robin Hood* had been falling badly. In fact, all the
actors wore anxious looks, Ben thought. It seemed
that desperate measures were needed. But glancing
at John again, Ben felt a surge of hope – for he had an
idea that his master had something up his sleeve.
Despite his cares, John had seemed more cheerful
this morning as they walked the short distance from
their house to the theatre. Ben waited.

"Very well, my friends..." John addressed the

whole company. "I wanted to tell you sooner, but I couldn't – not before everything was settled. But now I think it is. I was across the river yesterday, talking with Henslowe. I believe I have the solution to our troubles."

The others stirred. Philip Henslowe was a man of business who owned another theatre called the Rose, on Bankside, south of the River Thames. Southwark, as it was properly called, was known as a rough area. But a lot of people went there for amusements of one kind or another. The Rose had been built seven or eight years back, and was drawing big crowds. London's theatres just seemed to get busier and busier.

"Don't tell me we're moving across the river!" Will Sanders, the company's bookkeeper, was grumpy as usual. "I've just taken new lodgings, up the lane!"

"Let the man speak, master moaner." Hugh Cotton caught Ben's eye, and winked. It seemed he too had a notion that better news was on its way.

"Henslowe says he can give us a month's lease at the Rose." John paused to let his words sink in. "I know that'll be hard for some of you, crossing the river each day – or even moving lodgings…" He looked at Will. "But I don't think you'll mind too much, when you hear the rest of my tale."

There was silence. Now Ben saw that John was holding back a smile, and knew he had been right: a bigger surprise was coming. He felt a pang of excitement.

"Out with it, Master Symes!" Simon Jewell was finding it hard to bear the suspense. He was the best of the new actors the company had hired this winter: a stocky man with a beard trimmed to a dagger-point. But he was grinning at John. The others too had caught the whiff of good news. And now, with the air of a magician, John Symes reached inside his padded doublet and drew out an important-looking document. As he unfolded it, there were some sharp intakes of breath: at the foot of the document was the royal seal.

"It's from the Master of the Queen's Revels." John held up the paper. "Lord Bonner's players are ordered to play at Whitehall Palace, on December the twenty-sixth." His smile broadened. "So, a month's run at the Rose should give us plenty of time to work up a new play. What do you say?"

Ben gasped, as a stunned silence fell. Each year the Queen spent Christmas at one of her royal palaces – Whitehall, or perhaps Richmond or Greenwich – for twelve glorious days of feasting and entertainment. A company of players was always commanded to attend

– which meant a handsome fee, not to mention the thrill of performing in a splendid palace before the most important people in England. Until now, Lord Bonner's Men had never been called to play at the Christmas Revels. It was an honour that all the acting companies craved.

At once the players turned to one another, talking excitedly. Ben, who was standing near Solomon and Hugh, was about to speak – when he felt a sudden stab of pain in his side. But even as he whirled round, he knew what – or rather who – had caused it: Matthew Fields. Sure enough, he found himself face-to-face with his fellow boy actor: a blond, freckled lad who stood a couple of inches taller than Ben.

"What's the matter, Buttonhead?" Matt Fields seemed surprised. "You look like you've had a nasty shock."

But Ben's anger rose: he knew how good Master Fields was at playing innocent. "You stabbed me!" he said.

"Stabbed?" Matt looked puzzled. "You're letting your imagination run wild, Buttonhead—"

Then he broke off with a grunt, as Ben's hand shot out and grabbed him by the wrist. "I know it was you," Ben said. Despite being shorter, he was as strong as Matt. He was a country lad after all, and ever since he was seven or eight years old he had helped with the hardest of tasks, like harvesting. Now he watched Matt squirm as gradually his hand was forced upwards. Ben made him unclench it – and there in his palm was an iron brooch from one of the costumes Matt wore, with its pin open.

"Let go of me!" Matt flushed, and glanced round to see if anyone was watching. "I was only larking about, Buttonhead—"

"And stop calling me that!" Ben retorted. "Or I'll start calling you Fly-spot."

Now it was Matt's turn to get angry. The other boys at the last company he had belonged to, the Earl of Pembroke's Men, had mocked his dark freckles, saying it looked as if someone had swatted flies on his face. When Matt had joined Lord Bonner's company at the start of the winter, Ben had tried to make him welcome, and did not use his nickname. But that was before he and Matt decided they didn't like each other, which took less than a week. They had been at loggerheads ever since. Now Matt seemed to make life difficult for Ben, every chance he got.

"You call me that, and it'll be worse than a pinprick next time," Matt hissed. "You might find yourself tripping over onstage, and falling on your face in front of everyone!"

He wrenched his wrist from Ben's grasp – then without warning, with his other hand he seized Ben by the throat. Ben grabbed his hand and both boys began to struggle, no longer caring whether anyone noticed. Whereupon there was a shout, and a pair of strong arms clasped Ben from behind. Someone else took hold of Matt and pulled him away.

"Enough!" Hugh Cotton, who was holding Matt, frowned at Ben over the other boy's shoulder. "Are you two ever going to get along?"

Neither Ben nor Matt spoke. Solomon Tree, who was holding Ben, grunted in his ear, "What was it? Marian again?"

The players often joked about how Ben and Matt had fought hard for the best boy's part in *Robin Hood*: not the romantic role of Maid Marian, but that of the Sheriff's wife, which had the best lines. Ben had lost the argument and been told to play Marian. But like the professional he was, he took his part with good grace, and gave his best. Matt, on the other hand, instead of being grateful for his role, mocked Ben whenever they went onstage.

"It was nought, Master Sol," Matt said, meeting the tall comic's eye. "A bit of ribbing that got out of hand, is all…"

"What do *you* say?" Hugh Cotton was watching

14

Ben. He knew well enough who was likely to blame.

Ben looked hard at Matt. But it was not in his nature to tell tales, nor to expect anyone else to fight his battles. He gave his answer quickly.

"It's nothing. We were both overexcited – I mean, with playing for the Queen, and everything."

Hugh exchanged a glance with Solomon, before the two actors let go of Ben and Matt. Others who had been looking in their direction now turned away. The words *Christmas Revels* seemed to be on everyone's lips.

"Overexcited?" Solomon Tree's gloomy expression was back. "I don't know why. It's just another audience, royal or not." He brightened a little. "A new play, though… That's good. At least I won't have to act the fat friar much longer."

Ben took a couple of long breaths to calm himself, just as he always did before he went out on the stage. Turning away from Matt, he went to join the others in celebrating their good news. But as he walked towards John Symes, his master's earlier words struck him with such force that he stopped in his tracks. John saw him, and came forward.

"You look troubled – are you not pleased by the tidings?"

Ben nodded. "Of course I am! But I've just

remembered what you said, about us having to go to Bankside. We're not moving from Hog Lane, are we?"

For Ben, the worst thing about going on tour last summer was having to leave the old hound Brutus, as well as John's two lively daughters, Katherine and Margaret. Kate and Meg were like sisters to him now – or almost. He missed his real sister in Hornsey sometimes, as well as his younger brother and his mother. But John and Alice Symes and their girls were the closest thing to a family Ben had in London. The thought of having to leave them for a whole month dismayed him.

John smiled, and shook his head. "Let me set your mind at rest," he said. "I already talked it over with Alice, and she was outraged. To think we would both leave home and move south – it's out of the question. Anyway, Brutus would never let you leave!"

Ben gave a small sigh of relief, then saw that John's smile had faded. His master gazed into the distance, as if his mind were already drifting across London, to the south bank.

"No – we'll stay at Hog Lane," John said. "And make our way over the river each day by the Bridge, or by boat."

Suddenly he turned to Ben with a look of concern. "You've never been to Bankside, have you?"

"Only when we passed through, that day we started out on tour," Ben told him. "With Tarlton drawing the cart." Tarlton was the company's old chestnut carthorse, for when they went travelling.

"Well, I wager you'll get used to it," John said. "Only, it can be a dangerous place. Not much law and order down there, and some folk you'd do well to avoid." He sighed. "You'd best stick close to me or one of the others, to begin with."

Ben was quiet. He was thinking so hard about what John had said, he had almost forgotten Matt's cruel pinprick, and the pain in his side was disappearing. He glanced round to see the other actors talking cheerfully, and his heart lifted.

Perhaps he would not be playing Maid Marian much longer, after all. Instead there would be a new role, in a new play – and he would be performing at the famous Rose, where he had never been before. And if Bankside was really as wild and dangerous as people said it was…well, Ben had to admit that instead of scaring him, the idea excited him a little.

In fact, it sounded like the start of another adventure.

Chapter Two

There were times when it was almost impossible to cross London Bridge. Some days it was so crowded, with people going in and out of the shops and houses that lined the huge stone structure, you had to fight your way through. So, since there was no other bridge, many of those who wanted to get across the river went by boat. If there were several people, they might hire a wherry for a few pennies. But if there were only one or two, they could hire a one-man sculler for a halfpenny each. There were hundreds of watermen on the river, shouting and vying with each other for customers. On a busy day it was as noisy as a village football match. But that wasn't the reason Ben Button liked being on the water. It was because he might get the chance to ride in Jack Pike's boat.

Ben had stepped into Jack's boat for the first time a week ago, when Lord Bonner's Men had taken over the Rose Theatre. It was ten days since John Symes's announcement, and a great deal had happened. Some of the actors had found new lodgings on Bankside – like Will Sanders, since he was the company's bookkeeper and had a lot to do at the theatre. And though he grumbled about it, Ben knew that Will was pleased at the way things were shaping up. Who wouldn't be, when the theatre was full almost every day? It was the best thing that could have happened, everyone said. And now that the company was about to rehearse a new play for the Queen's Christmas Revels, there was much excitement in the air.

Jack Pike had never been to a theatre. The water was his home; in fact he was seldom seen anywhere else. He was an old man with a white beard, who wore a woollen seaman's hat and a heavy black jerkin. He often sat in his boat on the north side of the river, opposite the Falcon Stairs on the south bank where the players alighted for the theatre. When Ben and

John Symes first clambered into his little boat, the old waterman fixed Ben with a sharp eye, and said, "I've not seen you cross over to Bankside before, boy. What do ye do there?"

Ben was about to answer, but Jack shoved an oar hard against a post, sending his sculler shooting out onto the Thames. There was an ebb tide, and the river was grey and choppy. A cold spray hit Ben's face, making him gasp, and John Symes laughed aloud. Ben had to laugh, too. He turned to the waterman.

"I'm a player," he said proudly. "One of Lord Bonner's Men – we're playing for the Queen at Christmas!"

The other said nothing, but heaved on his oars. Finally, not sure whether he should speak or not, Ben gave his name and waited. And at last, just as he was wondering whether the old man had heard him, he received a reply.

"I'm Giacomo Pike, known on the river as Jack. I was dwelling on a few memories... I wager I had no more years than you, boy, when I first went to sea. Near fifty years back, it was – in the time of old King Henry." He sniffed, and pulled hard on his oars. "But then, you won't want to hear about that."

"You'd be wrong, master," John Symes said with a smile. "Ben here has enough curiosity to fill a barn!"

Jack turned his gaze upon Ben. But they were almost in the middle of the Thames now, and the wind was getting up. He looked behind to make sure he was headed in the right direction – which was just as well. A wherry was passing close by, and Master Pike had to slow his stroke to avoid it. Sitting in it were a couple of well-dressed young men in feathered hats and fur-trimmed cloaks, who called to him to look out. Their waterman shouted in a harsh voice.

"Have a care, Pike! Your eyes are failing – time you gave up your boat to a younger man!"

Ben frowned, but he did not know Jack Pike yet – for at once the old man flicked his oar skilfully, sending a shower of freezing river-water across the other boat's occupants. The young men cried out angrily as the spray splashed their fine cloaks, while the boatman cursed. Whereupon Jack tugged off his hat and waved it.

"Your pardon, sirs!" he called. "You'll forgive an old man's carelessness – seeing as his eyes are failing!"

The other boat was moving off now, and though the waterman shouted back, his voice was carried away on the breeze.

"There's not much wrong with your eyesight, Master Pike," John said. "Nor with your wits, from what I can see."

"Such folk don't trouble me," Jack muttered. But there was a twinkle in his eye as he pulled steadily on the oars.

Now the Bankside shore was drawing close. In the distance the round, timbered bulk of the Rose Theatre, with its flag flying high, loomed over the rooftops.

"So you're a player, boy...one of those as acts the woman. Do I hit the mark?"

Ben stiffened, looking keenly at Jack Pike. Some people scoffed at what he did – at what all boy actors did: play the female roles. Others disapproved, saying it was unseemly, even wrong, for boys to dress as women. But the next moment Ben was taken aback, for the waterman's face creased into a smile.

"To my mind, it takes a heap of courage to do that," he said. "And I wager you'd have made as good a sailor as Jack Pike, any day. I'm proud to have you in my boat."

After that, Ben could think of no reply. John smiled, but said nothing. Nor did any of them speak again, until the sculler glided up to the Falcon Stairs and bumped against the jetty. Then Ben was climbing out, and John was paying Master Pike for the trip, before he and Ben walked up the path to Bankside. Only at the top of the slope did Ben turn, to see the old man shoving his little boat out into the river. He did not look back.

That was a week ago. Ben had only been in Jack Pike's boat once more since then, and today he and John had crossed with another waterman. It was a Thursday – a cold and windy day, but an important one. For this was the day when Lord Bonner's Men would take delivery of a new play, which had been written specially for them.

There were a lot of people at the Rose that morning, leading players as well as others – the "hired men" who had been taken on for the new play. They gathered in front of the high stage that jutted out into the yard, a brightly dressed group, talking loudly. The Rose was round, like the other theatres, with three tiers of thatched galleries encircling the yard. It was not very big, but it could still hold more than two thousand people. When it was full, with everyone squashed together – especially those who paid just a penny to stand – the noise was deafening. The audience, men and women of all ages and all classes, were an unruly lot, often calling out rudely, and eating and drinking where they stood. Once or twice there had even been scuffles among them. Matt and Ben had been nervous the first time they stepped out of the tiring room onto the Rose stage. But in a short time, both boys had got used to the place. After all, apart from a couple of old plays they had revived to vary their performances, it was still *The Legend of Robin Hood* that they played most afternoons. And despite Ben's warning, Matt was still calling him "Buttonhead". There would have to be a reckoning between the two of them, Ben knew. He was getting tired of Master Fields.

Today, as he walked through the double doors with his master, he sensed how anxious the company were about the new play. Nobody knew whether or not it would do well – or even how good it was. But now it seemed there was something else going on, for Will Sanders was hurrying forward to speak with John. After the two men had talked in low voices for a minute, John called for attention.

"Will says there's a costume missing," he said. "And you all know how serious that is. It's the silver-lace doublet and the black velvet cloak edged with silver, that was passed on to us by Lord Bonner himself. It's worth nearly twenty pounds. Does anyone know anything about it?"

A silence fell. Ben could hear the watermen shouting from the river nearby. He knew as well as anyone that twenty pounds was a huge sum – as much as a hired man earned in a year. The costumes were the most valuable things the players owned. All the companies fined anyone who damaged or lost a costume – and it could take a long time to pay back the money.

Gabriel Tucker's moustache was bristling. "Surely you do not accuse us, John?" he cried. "You know none here would do such!"

It was true. Lord Bonner's Men had been through thick and thin together over the years. They were close friends as well as fellow players. Ben saw their anxious faces: Solomon Tree, mournful as ever, but one he would trust with his life; Hugh Cotton, who was like a big brother to him; Gabriel, who despite his sharp tongue would defend a friend to the death... Will Sanders, John himself – they were above suspicion. Even Matt Fields, Ben was sure, was not a thief. That left the new men: Simon Jewell, and the half-dozen other hirelings, who now stood about, looking worried. But the thought of any of them carrying out a serious theft, just when they had joined one of the best acting companies in England, seemed absurd. In fact, the same notion had occurred to John Symes.

"I do know it, Master Gabriel..." John sounded ashamed. He turned to Will. "Are you certain of this?"

"Of course I am!" Will growled. "I made a list of

our attire yesterday, for the new play." He spread his hands. "Though I still don't know what we'll need for that...and it seems our playmaker isn't here!"

There were some sighs. The playmaker was called Daniel Rix, and he was the most unreliable man Ben had ever known. He never arrived when he was supposed to – according to John, he sometimes vanished for days. Yet he was a famous poet, and he had promised to deliver his new play this morning. Everyone was counting on Master Rix – provided he turned up.

John raised a hand to quell the muttering. But one of the hired players stepped forward, a man with a red bushy beard and a large set of top teeth which jutted out over his lip. His name was Thomas Towne, but he was known all over London as Tom the Teeth.

"Master Symes – 'tis an outrage!" Tom the Teeth, like Gabriel Tucker, was also known for his short temper. "There's not a man here who wouldn't walk through flames for you and your fellows, as well as for the noble Lord Bonner – do you not know that?"

John was becoming exasperated. "Calm yourself, Tom," he answered. "I accuse no one! I merely ask if anyone has seen anything..." He trailed off, as stocky Simon Jewell moved up to put a calming hand on Tom the Teeth's arm.

"We understand, Master Symes," Jewell said. "And we'll all help search for the missing cloak and doublet." He sighed. "Yet there are thieves aplenty on Bankside – I know it only too well, for I've lived here most of my life. You must keep everything safe, and guard your valuables closely!"

John nodded, and was about to give instruction to Will Sanders, when there was a sudden commotion at the entrance. Everyone turned to see a shambling figure in a suit of mouse-grey taffeta and an old feathered hat hurrying through the doors. The man was breathless, his clothing awry, his hose baggy at the knees. His hair was long and untidy, while his brown beard was shaped to a long point like a church steeple. Seeing everyone looking at him, the fellow lurched to a halt and made a clumsy bow – which was a mistake, for the sheaf of papers he was carrying under his arm spilled over, and fell to the ground in a shower.

There was a gasp from more than a dozen throats. And in a moment, every one of Lord Bonner's Men had darted forward, as the pages of what they all knew was their new play began to scatter in the breeze. Soon they were running about the theatre yard snatching up the precious sheets, stumbling over one another in their haste. Ben stooped as one page floated past his feet, and managed to catch it. It was the title page. With growing excitement, he read the words:

The Witch of Wandsworth. Writ by Daniel Rix, Master of Arts. To be performed at the Rose Theatre, by the Lord Bonner's Players. Fortuna Favet Fortibus!

Ben looked up to see the playmaker himself coming towards him, fumbling with the papers he had managed to hold on to.

"Master Button – a thousand thanks," Daniel Rix murmured as he took the page from him. "It's the only copy, you know..."

There was an exclamation nearby. Ben glanced round to see John Symes walking over.

"The only copy!" John was alarmed. "What on earth possessed you to take such a risk, master?"

Rix shrugged. "Well...it's how I usually work," he muttered. "Paper is so expensive, you see..." He peered about, blinking. All over the yard, the players were gathering up the valuable pages of *The Witch of Wandsworth*. Luckily, no harm seemed to have been done. Will Sanders, grumbling under his breath, was collecting the sheets and putting them in order.

"What does that mean? *Fortuna Favet Fortibus*?" Ben asked the playmaker.

"Er...it's Latin," Rix answered. "I like to have a

motto, you see. It means 'Fortune Favours the Brave'."

Solomon Tree's lanky frame loomed up. The comic held out a couple of creased pages, which Master Rix took gratefully.

"The clown's role looks a bit thin," Solomon said. "Constable Clout – is that me? I'll have to spice it up a bit."

Solomon appeared glum, but the others knew him too well. Ben felt a smile coming on, and saw John begin to relax. Now he knew it: everything was going to be all right.

But that was in the morning; that night, everything changed. And though no one knew it yet, the loss of a cloak and doublet was only the start of the troubles that would befall Lord Bonner's Men.

Chapter Three

uring the night a fire sprang up. It started in a little thatched store-hut close to the theatre, containing old props and backcloths that were seldom used. But its cause was a mystery. The Rose stood on a patch of open ground beside a muddy way called Maiden Lane, which ran parallel to the river. There were no other buildings near. Not only that – the hut was old and rotten, its thatch mouldy and damp. There were no lights nearby – so how had it caught fire?

The first Ben knew of it was early in the morning, when he was woken by Brutus barking, then the voices of his master John Symes and John's wife, Alice. The next moment there were steps on the ladder which led to the small attic chamber where Ben slept. As Ben raised himself from his pallet, John's head appeared above the opening.

"Get up, quick!" he called. "There's a message from the Rose – we must go there at once!"

The room was icy, and Ben shivered as he dressed himself. But within a few minutes he was warming up, as he and John left the house and hurried along Bishopsgate Street towards the city wall. It was dawn, and there were still torches burning at the big stone gateway. But the doors had been opened, and the two of them were able to hurry through the arch, past the city guards. John ran at a steady pace so that Ben could keep up. But Ben was gasping for breath by the time the Bridge Gate loomed up out of the semi-darkness. A few minutes later, as Ben thought his lungs would burst, he and John were running past St Saviour's church on Bankside and turning left into Horseshoe Lane, named after its curving shape. Maiden Lane was ahead of them – but already they could smell the smoke. As they ran past the last house onto open ground, they heard shouts – and the cause of the uproar became clear. There was a little crowd milling about the store-hut, which was still smouldering. Ben came breathlessly to a halt, and saw men hurrying from the river with buckets to douse what was left of the building. Others had pulled the roof down with billhooks, and piles of charred thatch were scattered about. But as Ben watched, relief swept over him. For though the hut was ruined, it was clear that the fire had been contained. Only yards away, the Rose stood untouched.

A familiar face appeared, streaked with dirt. Will Sanders was coughing, but his relief too was plain as he walked forward to meet them.

"We were lucky the place was damp," he said. His voice was hoarse from breathing in smoke. "The fire was slow – though it had a strong hold by the time someone noticed it." He coughed again. "It's a good thing folk stay up late, hereabouts."

"It's a good thing the wind dropped, too," John said. "Thanks to that, the theatre was spared!"

They gazed at the ruined hut, which was still smoking. It was true: had the breeze been as strong in the night as it was the day before, it could have caught the flames and spread the fire to the Rose. With a shock, Ben realized how serious that would have been: all the company's costumes, their props, not to mention the building itself – everything could have been lost. It was almost too terrible to think about.

The three players stood in silence, watching men throw water over the smouldering ruins. But just then, there came a loud voice from behind them. They turned to see a heavy man in a tall hat and thick cloak striding towards them. After him shuffled a slighter figure with a wide-brimmed hat pulled down low. As the two men drew close, the taller one raised a finger and pointed.

"John Symes!" he cried. "I have a bone to pick with you!"

John stood his ground as the man walked up to him, still pointing. He was thin-faced, with a nose as sharp as a hatchet. Grey hairs poked out from under his hat, and from out of his ears too.

"I do not know you, sir," John began, but the other interrupted.

"But I know you!" he snapped. "I'm Henry Gilbert, alderman of this ward. And this is St Saviour's parish – my parish, that you theatre folk defile with your jigs and your play-acting! Now you see the consequences of your sinful ways – for what can this fire be, but an act of Providence?"

Ben was taken aback by the man's anger. His eyes blazed, while his hand trembled. The other man in the wide hat stood beside him in silence.

"Whatever the cause of the fire, alderman, I'm

certain it was an accident." John spoke calmly. "My company will clear up the site, and I'm sure our patron Lord Bonner will pay for what's been lost—"

"Your patron!" Alderman Gilbert almost spat the words out. "You and your company are but common players, fellow – rogues and thieves, fit for hard labour and little else!" The man drew a breath, and pointed at the Rose. "When Henslowe built that house of wickedness, I told him he would live to see it destroyed! I wish the fire had consumed it – every timber and all that's within! Then you could take yourselves back across the river to Shoreditch, where you belong!"

Will Sanders wiped his blackened face with a sleeve, and would have spoken up. But John Symes put a hand on his arm. Meeting Alderman Gilbert's gaze, he said: "I believe our patron will see things differently from you, sir. For in that house of wickedness, as you call it, we are rehearsing a new play for the Queen, to perform at the Christmas Revels. Why, even her chamberlain, Lord Hunsdon, has his company of players, which she delights in watching. Would you thwart the Queen's pleasure?"

At that, Alderman Gilbert almost exploded. "How dare you!" he cried. "I should have you and all your rabble arrested!"

He pointed to the man at his side. "This is Micklewright, constable of St Saviour's. I could have him put you in the stocks for your brazen speech! How would your patron like that?"

There was a short silence. Then, to the surprise of the players, the constable cleared his throat, gave a cough and said: "I doubt if that'll be necessary, alderman."

Gilbert swung round to face him. "What's that?"

"They've committed no offence that I can see," Constable Micklewright told him. "The fire was likely an accident, as this man says. As long as they behave themselves and don't make trouble with the other players, I see no difficulty."

"Other players?" John Symes looked puzzled. "What players are they, constable?"

The man pointed westward, towards the far end of Bankside.

"The new theatre – the Swan," he replied. "It's been completed. I hear the Earl of Horsham's Men have hired it." The man turned to Gilbert, who was seething with impatience. "There was small need to bring me here, alderman," he said. "You told me there was an affray – yet it's merely a hut burned down. Now if you'll allow, I shall return to my bed."

And with a glance at John, Ben and Will, the man turned and walked off.

The players watched him go. Here was a turnabout they had not expected. With relief, John faced Alderman Gilbert again.

"Will that be all, sir?" he asked. Without waiting for an answer, he continued, "Then with your leave, we will go and see what help we can be in clearing up the mess."

Gilbert was glaring at him. But after what the constable had said, there seemed nothing he could do. He was about to storm off, then suddenly he pointed again at John.

"Don't think you've seen the last of me!" he cried. "I'll be watching your company, every hour of every day! And at the first whiff of trouble, I'll bring the full weight of the law down on you. Let's see what your patron makes of that!"

Then at last he went away, disappearing round the corner of Horseshoe Lane.

Will Sanders was muttering under his breath. Seeing Ben's expression, he gave a snort. "Don't pay him any mind, boy," he said. "He's all wind and bluster, that one."

"I'm not so sure," John said thoughtfully. "I think we'll need to watch our step where Alderman Gilbert is concerned." Then he frowned. "Do you know anything about Horsham's Men taking over the Swan?"

"I've heard rumours," Will told him.

Ben was quiet. He had been thinking, as he listened to the alderman's angry outburst, that there was more to the man's rage than his disapproval of players. Then, realizing what John and Will had said, he looked up.

"I thought the Swan wasn't finished yet," he said.

Everyone knew about the new theatre on the south bank, that it was said would be a rival to the Rose. It was at the end of Bankside, near to Lambeth Marsh. But if another company of players had already moved in, it looked as if Lord Bonner's Men would have competition again, as they had done back at the Old Theatre at Shoreditch.

"It seems it is," John said. But he was relaxing. "At least they're not the Lord Chamberlain's Men," he added. "I don't think we've much to fear from Horsham's lot. They're as rough and ready a company as you'd find anywhere!"

"I heard they came back penniless after the summer," Will put in. "Had to borrow money to get by."

"Well, good luck to them," John said. "Are you

wide awake now?" he asked, turning to Ben. When Ben nodded, he went on: "That's well. If you ask me, there should be a bake-shop open somewhere – shall we take some breakfast, before we start work?"

For the first time, Ben realized how hungry he was, and gave a smile.

It was a long day, but an exciting one. The fire was out, and the ruins of the old store-hut were being cleared away. But by mid-morning, Lord Bonner's Men had forgotten all about it. For in a very short time everyone was so caught up in rehearsals for *The Witch of Wandsworth*, they could think of nothing else.

The Witch, as the players were now calling it, was turning out to be the best play Ben had ever been in. Daniel Rix had done the company proud. Indeed, he seemed as pleased with his new play as they were, and even turned up to watch them rehearse it. *The Witch* was about a poor old woman in the country village of Wandsworth, who was falsely accused of witchcraft by the wicked Sir Julius. Sir Julius really wanted her executed so that he could buy her cottage cheaply, because he believed there was a hoard of gold buried beneath it. And this time, to Ben's delight, he got to play the best boy's part – that of the witch herself. Matt Fields had to play the heroine, Lady Celia, who would fall in love with the hero, Adam Ardent.

Hugh Cotton of course was playing Adam, and would use his fencing skills, as he did in *The Legend of Robin Hood*. There was a battle in *Robin Hood* between the outlaws and the sheriff's men, which Ben always enjoyed watching, even though as Maid Marian he had to scream and look scared. When he started rehearsing *The Witch*, however, he grew excited: for he was secretly hoping he would get to do some sword fighting himself.

There was a fight near the end of the play in which nearly all the characters were involved. Since there were not very many actors, they had to change costumes quickly in the tiring room and hurry out again. And now that Ben had started having fencing lessons, he thought he might be included. When the company stopped work at midday for their dinner, he spoke to John Symes about it.

But John shook his head. "You're not ready," he said in a firm voice. "You've only just begun work with Master Bonetti – it's a dangerous business, stage fighting. Maybe in a month or two..."

"A month!" Ben was aghast. He had had two lessons with Carlo Bonetti at his fencing school in the

39

city, but already he had learned a lot. He pointed to where Tom the Teeth and the other hired men were standing, talking among themselves.

"Some of the hirelings aren't any better than me," he said. "They wave their swords about as if they were painting a wall – I heard Will say so myself!"

John looked away, but Ben saw now that he was hiding a smile.

"Because they know the risks," he said after a moment. "But in any case, they're in the background. It's Hugh and Gabriel the crowd want to see – players who can really do swordplay, and make it exciting. Don't you want to learn the proper skills, so that in time you can be at the front of the stage like them?"

Reluctantly, Ben nodded. He knew that John spoke wisely, as always. He walked away, trying to hide his disappointment.

One of the best things about leaving his home in Hornsey had been the thought that he would not have to go to the village school again. But, experienced player that he was, he was finding that there were still things he had to learn.

Sometimes, he wondered if they would ever stop.

Chapter Four

At the end of the afternoon, after another performance of *Robin Hood*, Ben walked down to the Falcon Stairs with John Symes. A blazing torch was fixed to a post by the jetty, but there was no boat waiting. So John called out "Eastward ho!", which was what people shouted if they wanted to go downriver. It was already dark and lights shone across from the city, glimmering on the water. Ben sat down on the bottom step, huddled in his jerkin. He was so tired, he could have slept where he was. All he wanted was a good supper and his warm bed in the attic.

There were footsteps from above. Ben and John looked up to see a figure emerge from the darkness. He was a handsome man with a neat beard, and as he walked down the stairs he broke into a smile.

"Master Mostyn." John held out his hand, but the other man paused before taking it. It seemed to Ben that he was not so friendly after all, though his smile remained.

"Master Symes…" The fellow's glance strayed towards Ben. "And who's this? One of your boy players?"

"My prentice," John answered. "Ben Button. Ben, this is James Mostyn, leading player of the Earl of Horsham's Men."

Ben got to his feet and made his bow. But meeting James Mostyn's gaze, he stiffened: there was a coldness in the man's eyes that seemed to spell a warning of some kind.

"I heard you'd taken over the Rose," Mostyn said to John. "And Rix has fashioned you a new play – is it so?"

John gave a nod, though he too seemed on his guard. "It's a fine piece," he said. "But what of you? We heard Horsham's Men were at the Swan. What are you playing?"

Mostyn shrugged. "*The Battle of Alcazar,* by

Master Peele." He sounded casual, but Ben saw that he was being careful with his words. His smile faded, and he put on a look of concern.

"We heard about your trouble," he said. "I trust no harm was done – to the theatre, I mean?"

"None." John met the man's eye. "Though we're puzzled at the cause of the fire."

"It must be very worrying," Mostyn agreed. Though he didn't sound very sympathetic.

Ben watched them both. It looked as if his master and this man were old rivals – even old enemies. But what was Mostyn hinting at?

Then, as if a cord had snapped, the tension between the two was broken. For there came a splash of oars, and a shout. The three turned to see a small boat appear out of the gloom. To Ben's delight, the waterman was Jack Pike.

"Master Ben!" Jack waved his old hat, jammed it back on his head, then gripped the jetty and pulled the boat close. Expertly he stood his oars on end and gestured to the players.

"I wager there's room for three," he called, "if Ben cares to squeeze himself into the bow…" He peered up at John Symes and Mostyn. "Will you come aboard, sirs?"

There was an awkward moment, but it was brief,

for Mostyn shook his head and stepped back. "I'll await my fellows," he said. "Besides, these good folk were before me..." With a grand gesture, the man waved John and Ben forward. Without further word, the two of them clambered into the sculler.

John did not look back. Instead he stared ahead as Jack Pike pushed the boat away from the jetty. The Falcon Stairs, and the leading player of the Earl of Horsham's Men, were soon lost in the dark.

Once they were on the river, with Jack rowing downstream, John relaxed. He began talking cheerfully with Master Pike, who liked to keep up to date with the news and gossip. And quickly the conversation turned to the blaze on Bankside, which it seemed everyone had heard about. But when John told the waterman that the fire was not serious, Jack became thoughtful. Ben was alert, for he had come to know the signs: it looked as if the old man was about to tell one of his stories.

"Well now...such a fire puts me in mind of that wicked practice they have, down in the West Country," Jack said. "You ever heard of *wreckers*, Master Ben? They who light false beacons on cliff tops, to lure ships onto the rocks below?"

Ben shook his head. It seemed a terrible thing to do.

"Aye..." Jack gazed into the dark as he spoke. "They're desperate folk as do such. Poor and desperate... They draw passing ships onto dangerous rocks, then, when they're holed and sinking, the wreckers swarm out and plunder the vessels – take everything! Why, 'tis even said they will drown survivors, if they have a mind to!"

John frowned. "It sounds a very cruel practice to me, Master Pike," he said.

"Indeed...you should be wary of false fire," Jack said, after a short silence. "For 'tis set to deceive you, and draw you in the wrong direction."

When John met the old man's gaze, he went on: "I may be wrong, Master Symes. Only from what I see, that little blaze you had was a blind. For if you can find no cause, how did it spring up – unless it was set by someone's hand? Have you pondered that?"

The thought of the fire being started on purpose had not occurred to Ben. The idea shook him – and when he recalled the tense conversation between his master and James Mostyn back on the jetty, he drew a sharp breath. And at once, he saw that John had had the same thought. For when he answered Jack Pike, his tone was severe.

"That's a grave accusation, master," he said, "and I will not dwell on it! And besides..." John seemed to be struggling for words, as if he were trying to convince himself. "Besides," he repeated, "even if someone wished to harm us, for some reason – Lord Bonner's players, I mean – why would they burn down an old hut, which held nothing of value? Surely they could have dealt a much harder blow, by setting fire to the theatre itself?"

But Jack Pike fixed him with a grim expression. "Aye…" He nodded slowly. "Perhaps 'twas a warning. Will you not dwell on that?"

He turned away and heaved on his oars. "As the old saying goes: *Beware false fire*, Master Ben," he muttered. "For 'tis the deadliest fire of all!"

Ben stared at him. He did not want to believe it. But somehow he knew that the old waterman spoke the truth.

The next day – Saturday – Ben awoke from a dream which he struggled to remember. There was fire in it, he recalled – which wasn't surprising. But there was something else…a noise – then as he sat up, he knew what it was: the sound of swords clashing. Today he would be late at rehearsal, for he had somewhere else to go. It was the day of his fencing lesson.

He was so excited as he dressed that he forgot all

about the fire. Nor did he notice the intensity of the light that came through his small window. In fact, it was not until he left the house that he saw what had happened, and stood blinking in the sunshine. For in every direction was an expanse of shimmering white. It had snowed.

With a spring in his step Ben walked down Bishopsgate Street, his shoes crunching the powdered snow. As he neared the gateway he heard shouts, and stopped on the corner of Houndsditch to watch a crowd of children having a snowball fight. He smiled to himself, and thought of home. He knew what his brother and sister would be doing, back in Hornsey village. He was tempted to join in the fun himself, but he had no time. Master Bonetti did not like to be kept waiting.

"Signor Ben – you here at last!"

The words greeted Ben a short while later, as he stepped out of the cold into Carlo Bonetti's fencing school. He was in a wide, bare room, behind the Bull Inn in Broad Street. There were benches around the walls, and above them hung enough swords to arm a small regiment. But these swords were not for soldiers: they were for fencers to practise with. Most of them were light rapiers, known as *tucks*. None was more than a yard long – the Queen had passed a law some years back making that the maximum length. Ben was learning with a small sword called a *foil*.

There were a few young men practising their skills at one end of the room. They took no notice of Ben, but Master Bonetti was beckoning him forward. Already he had taken down a foil for Ben to use. He was in loose breeches and shirt as usual, with a mail glove on his hand for protection. His wiry black beard bobbed under his chin when he spoke.

"Is a little heavier than you use last time," Carlo said, his dark eyes peering into Ben's. "Soon we make you a rapier-and-dagger man, eh?"

Ben liked Carlo Bonetti. He was Italian by birth, but had lived in London for many years. He was said to be the best fencing master in the city, though he had some odd methods. One was to make his pupils stand in a circle drawn on the floor, from which they were not allowed to move when they practised. Ben had once heard a young man ask if this was the Spanish method – whereupon Carlo had exploded with rage.

"*Sputo!* I spit on the Spanish! The Italian is the only way to fence, signor fool! The circle is so you learn to stand your ground, and not fall back. My old friend Rocco – the greatest fencer in England – used to make his pupils wear lead weights in their shoes, so they grew nimble. Maybe I make you wear them! Don't mention the Spanish to me again!"

Ben had been careful never to mention the Spanish method. Now he took the light sword from Carlo, walked into the circle and went into a fencer's crouch, with his right foot forward. He raised his left arm, extended his foil in front of him with his right, and made a lunge as if to strike an imaginary opponent – whereupon Master Bonetti gave a yelp of dismay.

"No, no! You not dancing! Your adversary may strike you – so!" Carlo had gone into a crouch himself and, with lightning speed, lunged so that his own foil struck Ben's chest. If its tip had not been blunted with a small cork, Ben would have been sorely hurt.

"You didn't give me a chance to ward, master," Ben said, a little breathlessly. "Didn't you say a gentleman would signal when he was ready to begin the bout?"

"*Si*, Signor Ben – but suppose one you fighting isn't gentleman?" Carlo wagged a finger at him. "A man must be ready to defend himself at any time. Especially if you work on Bankside now, at the *Teatro Rosa*!"

With a nod, Ben went back to his first position. It was true that there were a lot of rough characters on

Bankside, but he had not encountered any yet. Now Carlo was facing him, and there was a glint in his eye which made Ben concentrate hard.

"Well, Signor – now you will show me your *imbroccata*, and your *pararla*," the master said. "Your charging blow, and your warding blow. You ready?"

Ben signalled that he was, and tensed as he waited for his teacher to move. But at that moment the door flew open, bringing in an icy blast of air. With a look of annoyance, Carlo came out of his fencer's crouch and looked round.

Several people entered, talking loudly. Ben had mixed with theatre folk for long enough now to know that they were players. The men were dressed in brightly coloured clothes, and they moved with a cheerful swagger, knowing everyone was watching them. With them was a young fellow, close to Ben's age, though somewhat bigger than him. Ben guessed that he too was a boy actor. But this one was of a very different character from himself – and from Matt Fields too, in fact. For though Matt had some annoying ways, like playing cruel tricks on people, Ben knew that he was not a wicked lad. But this boy...

The newcomers were still talking and laughing. Then the boy looked round, and there was an expression on his face which Ben would not forget:

part sneer, part scowl. It was as if he despised everyone in the room – and more, as if he was daring them to challenge him.

Then his eye fell upon Ben Button. And Ben blinked, as if an invisible spark had been aimed at him. For as sure as there was snow outside, he knew that he had made an enemy.

Chapter Five

"His name's Edward Ratcliff – we used to call him Rat. He's with Horsham's Men now."

Matt and Ben were sitting on the edge of the Rose's stage, sharing a fruit pie for their dinner. The rehearsal for *The Witch* was over, and it would soon be time to get ready for their afternoon performance. The snow had been cleared from the theatre yard, and the midday sun was drying everything out. The players had found an iron brazier and made a fire of sticks in the middle of the yard. A group of them stood around it, talking and warming their hands.

In the gallery above the rear of the stage, musicians were tuning their instruments.

Ben had been telling Matt about the hard-faced boy he had seen earlier at the fencing school. But even before he finished describing him, Matt was nodding. It turned out that he and the other player had once worked together, as members of the Earl of Pembroke's Men.

"You didn't give him any offence, did you, Buttonhead? For if you did, you've made a big mistake!"

Matt was frowning, and for once Ben ignored the nickname. In his mind he saw the face of the one he now knew was Edward Ratcliff. He was taken aback to learn that "Rat" was one of the Earl of Horsham's players, who were performing nearby at the Swan Theatre.

"I never spoke with him," Ben said. "He stayed with his fellows while I had my lesson. He didn't look at me again."

"That's a bad sign," Matt said. "You must have done something to put his back up."

"I did not!" Ben was growing annoyed with Matt, as he always did. "He was the one staring around as if he'd like to try his *imbroccata* stroke on everyone in the room."

Matt almost choked on a mouthful of pie. "Oh – *imbroccata*, is it?" he retorted. "Pardon a plain fellow like me for not knowing what you fencers call it!"

Ben sighed. It was not his fault that the company had decided he should have fencing lessons first. Ben was younger than Matt, who had now turned thirteen, but he was a quick learner. John Symes had promised that Matt would have his turn, but that was not enough to satisfy Master Fields. Any opportunity he got, he would bring the matter up.

"You know well enough what I mean," Ben told him. "He looked like he was itching for a fight, and he didn't mind who with."

"Rat never does," Matt said. "And you'd better hope you don't run into him in the dark, because he's not fussy how he fights. He's as hard-nosed as they come. His father was a soldier, who beat him every day to toughen him."

Then Matt gave a snort of laughter, sending a shred of apple flying from his mouth. "I can guess what he'd think now if he was alive – to see his boy an actor, dressing in women's garb and speaking poetry!"

And he laughed at his own words, so that Ben too smiled at the notion. What Master Ratcliff looked like when he stepped out onstage in full skirts, he did not care to imagine.

*

That day Lord Bonner's Men performed an old favourite, *Doctor Faustus*, which always drew a crowd. The theatre was packed, but even the Rose audience were struck dumb with fear when Faustus the magician came to a terrible end for meddling with the powers of evil. When the play was over and the players took their bows, the applause was huge – a rousing chorus that shook the galleries. Ben, who had played the duchess, stood beside Matt, both of them tired but happy. This was the feeling Ben liked best in the world: the moment after he had given a good performance. And when he and the others left the stage and walked through the tiring-room door, even his fellow was inclined to be civil to him.

"Not bad, Button," Matt said, for once not using the annoying nickname. "You'll make a player one day."

Ben gave him a wry look. "So might you," he said.

The tiring room was crowded, and there was a buzz of voices as the actors began changing. Everyone was pleased with the performance – everyone, of course, except Solomon Tree.

"Call it a feeling," he said gloomily. "But I smell trouble… I smelled it today, before we started. First the missing costume, then the fire…" He shook his head.

Some of the players grinned behind Solomon's back – they knew all about his predictions of disaster. But just then Will Sanders came in, and seeing his expression, they fell silent.

"John wants everyone outside at once," he cried. "There's been another theft!"

The crowds had gone, and the company stood about on the stage as John Symes told them the grim news. Will had looked through the stock of attire again and made a discovery: there was not one costume missing this time, but two. Both of them were almost as valuable as the first one – which had never been found, despite a thorough search.

"The loss of the cloak and silver-lace doublet was bad enough," John said. "But now the saffron suit for Sir Julius is gone – and the lilac gown with the gold thread for Lady Celia. These are clothes we cannot afford to lose – for as you know, *The Witch of Wandsworth* opens on Monday!"

Nobody spoke. Matt looked stunned: the Lady Celia costume had been made especially to fit him by the company's tailor. He and Ben exchanged glances. Ben was relieved that at least his witch's costume was safe. But he knew now, with three costumes missing, that this was no mischance. The players looked at one another, all thinking of Will Sanders' words in the tiring room: there seemed no doubt now that there was indeed a thief about.

But no one could shed any light on the matter, and soon afterwards John dismissed the company. Everyone promised to be alert and watch out for anything suspicious. Meanwhile they would have to alter some old costumes for Lady Celia and Sir Julius. The constable, Micklewright, would be told. The theft of such valuable items was a serious felony.

It was growing dark as Ben and his master left the theatre with Matt, Simon Jewell and Tom the Teeth. The players walked along Maiden Lane, saying little, for the loss of the costumes troubled them all. But Ben had had a thought, and could keep it in no longer.

"The more I think on it," he said, "the more certain I am that Master Pike was right: the hut fire was a warning."

"A warning of what?" Simon Jewell turned sharply to him.

Ben was looking at his master. He knew that John too remembered what Jack Pike had said to them the day before. Now, it did not seem so fanciful. After a moment John slowed his pace, then stopped.

"It's possible that someone might want to make things difficult for us," he said.

"Difficult?" Tom the Teeth was frowning. "You mean—"

"He means someone wants to put us out of business." Simon Jewell, it seemed, had been thinking along the same lines as Ben.

"I know you don't like to accuse folk, Master Symes," Simon went on. "So let me spell it out. We all know there's a company of players, not far from where we stand now, who'd gladly see us pack up and go back to Shoreditch. Because not only do we draw bigger crowds, we're better than them, and they know it! More, they're a rough lot, who wouldn't stop at a few mean tricks—"

"Enough, Master Jewell!" John sounded unhappy, but Ben knew he was not angry. He remembered the expression on John's face as they sat in Jack Pike's boat – and before, during the encounter with James Mostyn. And he knew now that John too suspected the Earl of Horsham's Men. It was an unpleasant thought, but it had to be faced.

"Even if it's true..." John spread his hands helplessly. "Even if they want to take our audience – and we know how tough the competition is in our profession – what proof have we?" He shook his head.

"Setting buildings alight, let alone stealing valuable costumes – those are desperate acts! I cannot accuse Mostyn and his fellows of such crimes!"

"There's one I would accuse, Master Symes."

Matt had been silent. Now he faced John – and even before he spoke, Ben guessed the name that would be on his lips.

"Edward Ratcliff."

Simon Jewell gave a start. "I know him," he said. "He's only a lad, but he's a hard one, all right…"

"But would he go this far?" Tom the Teeth asked, in an uneasy tone. "Would even he be so reckless as to risk the gallows?"

After a moment John shook his head. "It seems foolhardy."

He drew a deep breath, and eyed each of his players. "Well – mark this: whoever our foes are, if they wish to drive Lord Bonner's Men out of Bankside, then I say they have failed! We've faced worse and survived – and besides, we have a new play to perfect before we show it to the Queen. Is that not something to cheer about?"

The others brightened at once. It was true: Bonner's were the best – so long as you didn't count the Lord Chamberlain's Men. Ben saw that Matt too was reassured. And now Simon Jewell was grinning.

"Well said, Master Symes!" he cried. "I'll wager a week's pay that *The Witch* will be the best play seen at Whitehall in years. And I hear that if the Queen's pleased with a performance, she showers the players with gold – is it not so? We'll all be rich!"

There were smiles, and the players fell into step again. They turned into Horseshoe Lane where there were lights. Simon Jewell stopped and pointed.

"The Elephant's the best inn on the south bank," he said. "Who'll join me in a mug of ale?"

Tom the Teeth seemed eager, but John Symes hesitated, and Ben knew that his master was thinking of him. Though Ben had been inside taverns before, he knew that those in Bankside could be dangerous places. But John deserved a drink with his fellows, to cheer himself up – and Ben did not want to deny him.

"I'll wait for you," he said. "Master Fields and I will wander down to the river…" He turned to Matt. "What do you say?"

Matt hesitated for barely a second. "I'm with you," he said.

And so it was settled. Promising to come and find Ben in half an hour, John and the other two players walked off towards the Elephant. Whereupon, suddenly aware that they were free to go where they liked, both boys grew excited. And neither of them paid much heed to John's warning not to go far but to stay close to the Bridge. In a moment the two of them were hurrying down to the riverside.

They passed the famous Winchester House, home of the Bishop of Winchester, who owned most of the land on Bankside. On their left, a big, somewhat grim-looking building loomed. As they skirted its walls, Ben glanced curiously at it.

"That's the Clink – the worst prison there is," Matt said.

"Why is it the worst?"

Matt shrugged. "Just take it from me," he said quietly, and walked on.

Ben's curiosity was aroused, but he said nothing further as the two of them emerged between two houses to halt at the riverside. Across the Thames, lights showed from the city, and as always the watermen were shouting in the distance. Despite the chill and the growing dark, Ben and Matt were ready for some entertainment of their own. Their eyes met, they backed away from each other…and in an instant both were stooping and scraping snow together, hurrying to see who would be first. To Ben's misfortune, it was Matt.

The snowball caught Ben full on the nose, making him gasp. But at once he patted his own missile together and hurled it. Matt ducked and managed to avoid it, but as he straightened up Ben was already fashioning another. This time his aim was true, and it was Matt who was gasping as he wiped wet snow from his brow. He bent quickly and scooped up more snow, and as he did he called out.

"A lucky throw, Button! Now prepare to get drenched!"

Ben was laughing to himself, thinking of what he had seen on the corner of Houndsditch that morning: he had managed to get into a snowball fight after all. He was moulding another ball, alert for Matt's next move, when there came a sound from somewhere to his right. He looked up and saw Matt standing dead still, staring at a gap between houses. And at once, Ben froze too.

Three boys had appeared, trotting towards them. There were no snowballs in their hands – instead they carried stout wooden sticks. And instinctively Ben and Matt moved close together, both realizing what they faced. The trio drew nearer, so that their faces became visible – whereupon Ben heard Matt utter a groan.

Their leader was the swaggering boy from the fencing school, "Rat" Ratcliff. And he was wearing a triumphant smile.

Chapter Six

It was the most desperate fight Ben had ever been in.

The three boys did not speak. They simply fanned out into a line and, as they advanced, began swinging their wooden billets. Ben tensed in every muscle – then glanced at Matt, who stood with a snowball still in his hand. Quickly Matt spoke from the side of his mouth.

"Watch the skinny one – leave Rat to me!"

The boy running towards Ben was indeed a thin rake of a fellow. And the next thing Ben knew, a billet was slicing through the air towards his head.

Ben had always been quick on his feet. He ducked fast, so that the weapon whistled past his ear. Without thinking he snatched it – and to his surprise it flew out of the boy's grasp. The boy made a grab for it – then cried out, for Ben had swung it and given him a sharp crack on the elbow.

But the success was short-lived, for Ben and Matt were outnumbered. Even as Ben turned from his first assailant, he saw Rat launch himself bodily at Matt, the two of them falling heavily into the snow. Then they were grappling furiously, each trying to get hold of the billet. And for the first time, one of them spoke.

"Smash the Cherry-tops! Hammer them into the ground!"

It was Rat who was doing the shouting. By "Cherry-tops", Ben guessed he meant the crimson doublets Ben and Matt wore. Now the third boy, a dark fellow with long, greasy hair about his face, was coming fast at Ben. Ignoring the one he had hit, Ben dropped into a crouch and faced his new opponent. But this boy was more cunning. Instead of using his stick, he fetched Ben a brutal kick on the shin. The pain was sharp, but Ben managed to swing his stick – only to meet with empty air. And too late he heard the sound behind him. The next moment he was seized.

The skinny fellow had him by the arms – and he was shouting with rage.

"Go for his face, Gaddy!"

Fear rose in Ben's heart. He realized that these fellows – whom he guessed were Horsham's boys, like Rat – wished him real harm. This was no casual scuffle between rival players: it was a fight for survival.

But his thoughts sped by in a second. He heard Matt cry out, and guessed that he was losing his battle. There seemed to be no one else near; Ben was on his own. Breathing hard, he faced the worst. And Carlo Bonetti's words from the fencing school that morning flew suddenly into his head: *Suppose one you fighting isn't gentleman?*

The long-haired boy called Gaddy was clearly no gentleman. Both his fists whirled, and even Ben's reactions weren't quick enough. The first caught him a stinging blow on the left cheek, the second thudded against his right eye, and for a moment everything went hazy. Gasping, Ben tried to focus... He saw the boy raise his fists again, while behind him the other held his arms tight. Ben was struggling wildly now – then suddenly, a memory from home welled up. He was fighting a village bully on the green, with his friends shouting to encourage him – and at once he knew what to do. With all his strength he jabbed his right arm backwards, and slammed his elbow into the skinny boy's stomach.

There followed a loud gasp, and for a second the grip on Ben was loosened – which was all he needed. Wrenching himself from the other's hold he twisted away, as Gaddy's fist came flying at him again. But this time he missed, for Ben had ducked low. And when his attacker's momentum carried him forward, Ben seized his chance. As hard as he could, he brought his own fist upwards to crack his opponent under the chin.

There was a grunt of pain, and Gaddy staggered. His mouth fell open and blood ran out. Then, with a surprised expression, he sat down in the snow and put a hand to his face.

But there was no time to waste. Ben whirled round as the skinny one lunged at him. The next moment however, the tables had truly turned – for Ben still held the billet. And now his arms were free.

"Cherry-tops – is that what you called us?" Ben shouted. "Well here's something to remember the Cherry-tops by!"

And giving free rein to his anger, he cracked the skinny boy on the shins. Then he was swinging wildly, finding the fellow's arms and shoulders. Furiously he wielded the billet, heedless of where it landed. Then he stopped – for all at once the other turned and ran off howling, to disappear between the houses, the way he had come.

Breathlessly, Ben looked round. He had been aware of cries and scuffling only a few yards away. Now he saw Matt on his back, hurt and bleeding... and standing over him was Rat. And as Ben watched, the club rose in the air...

But Rat never delivered his cruel blow, for the speed of Ben's charge caught him by surprise. The hard-faced fellow had barely time to look round before Ben's billet fell upon his shoulder with a thud. Rat cried out, and dropped his own stick. To Ben's relief he stepped backwards – long enough for Matt to roll away. Breathlessly he scrambled to his feet, and quickly picked up Rat's weapon.

Bruised and panting, Matt and Ben stared at Rat. But the danger had passed. Swiftly Rat took in the situation: one of his companions had fled, the other was sitting in the snow, holding his bloodstained chin. For a moment, the villainous fellow eyed his foes. Then he spoke in a cold, rasping voice.

"Luck smiled on ye this night, Bonner's boys. Next time she will not! For no one beats Edward Ratcliff, without payment in full!"

The boy winced with pain and gripped his shoulder, before turning his gaze upon Ben. And the hatred in his eyes would have made even a stout man quail.

"You'll get what's coming to you, Button!" he said. "Then you'll be slinking back across the river where you belong – if you can still walk, that is!"

Ben raised his club and made as if to step forward – but there was a murmur from close by. Ben looked round, and saw Matt shake his head. So the two of them remained still as Rat went over to Gaddy, seized him by the arms and dragged him to his feet. Then both boys were walking away, to disappear between the houses.

Ben and Matt watched them go, before turning wordlessly to each other. They were hurt, but they had triumphed against the odds. Around them, the snow was spotted with drops of blood.

Slowly and stiffly, the two victors began to walk back towards London Bridge.

The next morning, Ben was in more trouble – not from his master John Symes, but from John's wife, Alice. For when she learned what had happened to him, she flew into one of her famous tempers.

"Cherry-tops, is it? Well your new red doublet's a mess! And now you've got a cherry-coloured cheek, and a black eye to go with it! I've a mind to send for a barber-surgeon and have him lance the swelling – how would you like that?"

She sat by Ben's pallet in the attic, bending over him sternly. She was a round-faced woman with large eyes and, with her dark hair swept back and pinned, she always looked severe. Fortunately Ben knew her for the kind soul she was, though he winced while she dabbed witch hazel on his bruises. It was the Sabbath, and luckily there was no performance. Indeed, when John and the other players had seen the state of Ben and Matt the previous night, it was at first doubtful whether there would be a performance the next day either. Only when the boys swore that they would be fit to play did John agree that *The Witch of Wandsworth* should open as planned.

There were footfalls on the ladder, and John's head appeared. But before he could speak Alice turned to glare at him. "Don't think you're forgiven, John Symes!" she snapped. "Leaving your prentice alone on Bankside, while you roistered in a tavern! What on earth were you thinking of?"

John climbed the steps to stand sheepishly in the middle of the floor. Despite the ache in his leg, which was badly bruised, Ben wanted to laugh. John never looked forlorn, except when Alice was angry with him.

"How are you feeling?" he asked.

"I'm well," Ben told him. "I'll get up soon, and—"

"Will you now?" Alice sat back on her stool. "Hear this, master brawler: you'll get up when I'm satisfied you're well enough, and not before." She frowned suddenly. "You didn't get cracked on the skull, did you?"

"They're only bruises," Ben said, with a shake of his head. He looked anxiously at John. "I think Matt took worse injury than me. Is there any news?"

John nodded. "Will went to see him first thing this morning," he said. "He's got a cut mouth and bruised ribs, but his mother says he's well enough to get up."

Ben was relieved. Sitting propped up with a bolster as he was, he felt ashamed to be fussed over. And fond though he was of Alice, he was glad when she got up and went downstairs. John waited until he and Ben were alone before sitting down beside the pallet.

"Is there something else wrong?" Ben asked, seeing his master's grave expression.

John sighed. "You know what this means?" he asked. "It means open war with Horsham's Men."

Ben stared at him.

"I thought it was coming," John went on, "even before Simon Jewell spelled it out – ever since I spoke with James Mostyn, by the stairs. He and I go back a long way. We're a threat to his company, and they want us out of Bankside. And now this."

His master looked anxiously at Ben's bruised face, and shook his head. "Thank heaven it wasn't worse," he went on. "We can cover up your bruises – Will Sanders has a good remedy for such: white lead and vinegar. From a distance, nobody will notice."

But Ben's mind was on other things. He had lain awake for much of the night, thinking – about the fire, but especially about the thefts. And now seemed as good a time as any to venture his opinion.

"I know you can't accuse Horsham's men of stealing, or of setting fire to the hut," he said. "But what if we found some proof? Like, how they managed to take the costumes, when Will keeps them locked in the tiring room…"

"What do you mean?" John was frowning. "You think there's a traitor in our company?"

"Is it possible?" Ben asked, after a moment.

His master looked unhappy. "I refuse to believe it," he replied. "I know Bonner's Men, and I would trust them to the death. Even the hired men – I've known most of them for years. They're players, who want no other life. They may be mischievous folk at times, but they would never do anything to harm us. I would swear to it."

Both of them were silent for a while. Ben knew that his master spoke the truth. But something was nagging away at the back of his mind. He wished heartily that he knew what it was.

"Well – enough!" John was brisk all of a sudden. He patted Ben on the arm and stood up. "You're not as badly hurt as I feared – nor is Matt, and I'm much relieved. I thought the worst, last night... I should never have let you go off. So mind what I say: you mustn't walk alone after dark, anywhere on Bankside. Do you promise me?"

Ben promised, and soon afterwards John went downstairs.

Lying back on his pallet, Ben thought hard about what his master had said. He wondered what open warfare with the Earl of Horsham's company might mean...more thefts, or something even worse? From downstairs, he heard voices. If Alice did not come back soon, he resolved to get up anyway and show her he was well. He could offer to cut some wood for the fire...then he might take Brutus out for a walk.

But before he knew it, he had fallen fast asleep.

By the following afternoon, all thought of his injuries had been pushed firmly to the back of Ben's mind, when the trumpet rang out from the little platform above the Rose's stage, and *The Witch of Wandsworth* opened to a packed theatre. And from the very start, he knew it would be a day to remember – even if things did not turn out as he had expected.

All had gone well until the last few minutes of the play – the big sword fight. Since they were not included, Ben and Matt stood behind the tiring-room door in their costumes, watching through the gap. And Ben had to admit that it looked dangerous. The hired men were doing lots of shouting as they waved their swords about and, despite Will Sanders's misgivings, they looked fierce enough. But it was Hugh Cotton and Gabriel Tucker that everyone watched. For this time, the two players excelled themselves. Hugh, as the hero Adam, and Gabriel, as the wicked Sir Julius, leaped about the stage with great energy. And though Ben knew how carefully they had rehearsed their moves, he was as caught up in the fight as were the audience – *oohing* and shouting, cheering every time one of Sir Julius's men went down. For of course the hero would win, as sure as it was winter and there was snow outside.

At last only three swordsmen remained on their feet. With a triumphant shout, Adam Ardent dealt Sir Julius the death blow, and down went Gabriel with a cry of agony. Then Hugh, as Adam, turned to despatch the last of the bad men. He was played by Tom the Teeth, who had been waving his sword with gusto. When Hugh thrust under his arm, it really looked as if Tom had been stabbed. Giving a roar of pain, Tom toppled over and lay still, to a few cheers from the crowd. Ben and Matt were sorry the fight was over – or so they had thought. Because now, something unexpected happened.

It seemed there was another hired man on the stage, whom Ben had not noticed before. He was a short, stubby fellow with brawny arms, who had somehow kept in the background during the fight scene. Now, to Hugh's surprise, the man stepped forward – and Ben went rigid. He knew that something was very wrong; for at once the man dropped into a real fencer's crouch.

Hugh hesitated, knowing this had not been rehearsed. Then, thinking that some mistake had been made, he tried to cover it up. Giving a shout, he raised his sword – but that was all he did. And then it seemed to Ben that everything slowed down, as if it were an eerie dream.

He saw – as everyone else saw – Hugh Cotton, his handsome face glowing, sword uplifted. He saw his opponent lunge…an *imbroccata*, Signor Bonetti would have called it. And Ben gave a cry – for he saw too that there was no cork on the tip of the man's sword; nothing to stop it as he drove it into Hugh's chest.

Hugh did not fall over and play dead, as the others had done. His arm dropped, his sword fell to the stage with a clatter, and he sagged to his knees. And someone in the crowd screamed…for at last it was clear what had happened. The leading player of Lord Bonner's Men had really been stabbed!

And before anyone could stop the culprit, the fellow ran across the stage and disappeared into the tiring room. Ben and Matt had barely time to get a look at him as he brushed past, shoving them both aside.

Then, in a moment, he had vanished.

Chapter Seven

*I*t was a miracle, everyone said, that Hugh had not been killed.

He lay on the floor of the tiring room, his head resting on a rolled-up cloak. The company clustered about him while Will Sanders kneeled at his side, pressing a cloth to the wound. Hugh's white linen shirt was soaked with blood, but he was conscious. By sheer luck, Will said, the attacker's rapier had struck one of Hugh's ribs. It had missed his heart by less than an inch, which shocked everyone. For it was now clear that the stubby man had meant to take his victim's life – there onstage, in front of the entire audience.

The constable had been called. So had a barber-surgeon, and it was an anxious time for the company as they waited. But to everyone's relief, Hugh did not lose consciousness. He was even able to speak.

"Who was that fellow who ran me through?" he asked weakly. "I've never seen him before."

Nobody had an answer. They had been asking themselves the same question, only to discover that no one knew the man. In the excitement before the play, with the players hurrying to get ready, none had noticed that there was an extra man – a stranger – in the tiring room. Even Will Sanders, who handed out the swords to the hirelings, had been too busy to pay attention. And no one saw the man remove the stopper from the end of his foil. Whoever he was, he was as bold and cruel a villain as could be imagined.

Ben and Matt had been questioned by John, but neither of them could tell him much. Like everyone else, they had been too shocked by events to try and stop the man as he pushed past them. There was a narrow door at the back of the tiring room, and a flight of steps which gave onto open ground behind the theatre. It was the side nearest the river, and that was how the fellow must have made his escape.

He could have run down to the waterside and taken a boat.

There was a stir as the barber-surgeon arrived at last. He was a white-haired man in a black gown and skull cap, and the first thing he did was order everyone to leave. So, in silence, the company went out to the stage. There they gathered around John Symes, wondering what was going to happen next.

Ben and Matt had barely spoken since the terrible event. Matt had recovered well from the fight two days ago. His bruises and the cut on his lip were hidden under the white lead paste Will had daubed on him. As for Ben: for his role as the witch, his cheeks and his black eye were painted over, and he had not yet had time to clean it off. Now the two boys stood close together. Neither said anything – but it was clear that something had changed between them. They had faced danger together, and overcome it. Perhaps, Ben thought, they were no longer such enemies. Were they even friends?

The galleries were now empty, though a few curious folk lingered in the theatre yard. But when a man in a cloak and wide-brimmed hat came through the open doors, people began to move away. Ben looked down, and recognized him at once: Micklewright, the constable. And one glance was enough to know that he was angry. Pushing through the onlookers, he walked to the stage and looked up at John.

"I stuck up for you after the fire, Master Symes," he said. "I said I'd leave you be, provided there was no trouble. Yet you've been here only ten days, and already it seems I have a feud in my parish!"

John did not answer at once. He moved to the edge of the stage, bent, and dropped lightly to the ground. Then he faced the constable squarely.

"If there's a feud it's not of our making, constable," he said. "We've done no wrong – indeed we're the victims: of theft, and now of serious wounding. Our leading player is lucky to have escaped with his life!"

Micklewright frowned. "I'd think carefully if I were you, before you go accusing folk of such offences," he said. "That's a hanging matter!"

"I know it," John replied. "But when you hear the whole tale, you'll find there's no mistake. Someone – a stranger – wormed his way into our company, and tried to—"

Then abruptly John fell silent. His eyes were on the doors, where another figure had appeared. The players followed his gaze – and Ben's heart sank. Like the others, he could only watch as Alderman Gilbert strode into the middle of the yard. And even before the alderman's words were out, Lord Bonner's Men guessed what would happen. Wearing a sour smile, the man halted and held up an official-looking document. Then he made his announcement in a loud voice.

"This theatre is now closed!" he cried. "I have an order signed by members of the Privy Council. There will be no performances until further notice!"

A few hours later, after dark, a meeting took place not far away, in a back room of the Elephant tavern.

There were six people present: John Symes, Will Sanders, Solomon Tree, Gabriel Tucker, and Ben and Matt. Hugh Cotton, having been treated by the barber-surgeon, had been taken to his lodgings to rest. The hired men, even Simon Jewell and Tom the Teeth, were sent home by John, with his regrets and a little money. How long it would be before the theatre opened again was anyone's guess. All players faced such times – it was one of the hardships of their profession. But after performing an exciting new play like *The Witch*, only to have it end in such a terrible way, being thrown out of work was hard to bear. All of the hired men wore sad expressions as they said their farewells in Maiden Lane. But as the regular company watched them go, they sensed that John Symes had more to say to them. Within minutes he had steered them into the Elephant and asked the landlord to let them have a private room. Here they sat round a table to decide what to do – and it was not long before the meeting became a council of doom.

"These are the facts, my friends – you may turn them about as you will." John was tired, and his face was taut. "First, the money: we can't perform, yet our lease of the Rose stands. I still have to pay Henslowe the rent – not to mention our wages."

Nobody spoke, for this much they knew already.

"Second: though the constable says he'll look into the matter of Hugh's wounding, I've little faith in the man. So I've sent word to Lord Bonner. He trusts us, yet I fear he'll be displeased when he hears what's happened. He would want no bad blood between us and another company—"

"But we didn't start it!" Gabriel Tucker's moustache, which he had kept for his role as Sir Julius, was twitching fiercely. "It's Horsham's Men! From the moment we came here they've wanted to get rid of us. Everyone knows it!"

"Well – even if it's so, we can't prove it," John

replied. "I know Mostyn well. He'll deny knowledge of any wrongdoing – especially the attack on Hugh. And it could be that he knows nothing of that. For whoever that fellow was who posed as one of our men, he's no player, or I would have recognized him."

John was looking worried now. "No...what I fear most is that our performance at the Queen's Revels may be cancelled."

There was a gasp from every throat. The players looked at each other in dismay. Here was something none had considered.

"Why should that be?" Solomon Tree had been staring mournfully into his mug of beer. "We still have the lease on the Rose. If we can't perform, then at least we can rehearse. We can practise *The Witch* until it's perfect."

"Except for one thing: we've no leading player." Will Sanders looked round at the anxious faces. "The surgeon says Hugh has taken serious hurt," he went on. "He won't be able to go onstage again for days – perhaps weeks. And even then, he won't be fit enough to do swordplay."

Ben exchanged looks with Matt. He had been so relieved that Hugh was not mortally hurt, he had not thought about what his loss would mean.

"I know it, Master Will," John said. "I see only one solution: I shall have to take over the role of Adam myself. A good hired man could take my part as Farmer Wandle, and the rest may be changed around to fit."

The others brightened, but John's face remained grave. "No – that isn't our main difficulty," he went on. "Our main difficulty is Alderman Gilbert."

At the mention of that name there were groans, and Gabriel Tucker startled everyone by banging his fist on the table. "That hard-faced killjoy!" he cried. "From the very start he's wanted to close us down. And why, I ask? Why does he pick on us?" He turned his fierce eye upon John. "We've all known Puritans like him," he said. "The man disapproves of plays and players, as such folk disapprove of anyone having a little fun! Yet does he threaten Horsham's Men, as he threatens us? Have you thought on that?"

There was a silence, so that the tavern noise could be heard through the wall: loud voices, laughter, even singing. Though the players barely noticed it, for each was pondering Gabriel's words. Ben too kept his thoughts to himself. He remembered how he had felt when he first saw Alderman Gilbert on the night of the fire. And somehow, he knew now that there was more to this than a feud between two rival acting companies. There and then, he made himself a promise: to help John and his fellows by trying to find out what was really behind the disasters that had befallen Lord Bonner's Men.

He looked round as Matt spoke up. The boy was unable to hide his disappointment, for despite his cocky ways everyone knew how much he wanted to play before the Queen.

"I don't understand," he muttered. "Surely even Alderman Gilbert can't stop us playing at the Christmas Revels?"

"Perhaps not," John answered. "Yet he seems to have taken against us for some reason. And now that Micklewright too is angry with us, it wouldn't be hard for Gilbert to have him arrest a few of us, if he can claim we've broken the law. Even if we can go on without Hugh, we can't afford to lose any more players."

It was a grim thought. But now, to Ben's relief, his master sought to rally their spirits. "I say he will try," he went on. "I do not say he will succeed. We can still rehearse, as Solomon says. We can learn some new songs too, for the Queen's delight. And if we work behind closed doors, even Gilbert cannot make much objection, provided we keep out of his way – and out of trouble, of course."

Now he looked at Ben and Matt. "That means our prentices too. No more fighting with Horsham's boys!"

Ben and Matt kept silent. They knew, as the others knew, that the fight with Rat, Gaddy and the other boy had not been of their making. But they understood what John was telling them.

Now, it looked as if all had been said. But before anyone got up to leave, John held his hand up once again.

"There's one other thing we can do," he said. "We can go to the Swan tomorrow, and speak to Horsham's Men."

No one expected that. There was an intake of breath, before John went on. "We'll all go together," he said. "We'll carry a flag of truce, and we'll threaten nobody – but we'll go in boldly, and have it out with them. I want no feud – Mostyn must understand that. We have no proof, so we'll make no accusations of theft, or of arson – let alone attempted murder. Yet we'll make it clear that Lord Bonner's Men will not be broken!"

Ben's heart lifted, and he knew the others felt the same. Even Solomon Tree and Will Sanders grinned, while Gabriel thumped the table again for good measure. But before Ben could speak, Matt Fields spoke up for the two of them.

"I trust you won't leave the boy players out," he said. "For have we not earned the right to be there, too?"

"So long as you heed my words, and stay back," John said. "I mean it: I want no trouble."

Will gave one of his grunts. "That's well," he said. "With the boys, we make six – enough for a proper embassy."

"Yes…but seven's a better number, Master Sanders."

Nobody had heard the door open. At the sound of another voice, everyone turned in surprise to see the last person they expected: the playmaker, Daniel Rix.

"It's…well, it's my best piece, you see…" Rix shuffled nervously into the room. In his hand was a cup of wine, half of which he managed to spill on the floor. Summoning a glassy smile, the author of *The Witch of Wandsworth* faced John Symes.

"The fact is," he murmured, "I've set my heart on seeing the play done before the Queen's Majesty. I would hate for anything to spoil its chances…and not only that: there's no other company in all England that I would have perform it. For none could do it better than Lord Bonner's players. So, er, I think I should come with you tomorrow…if that's all right?"

Rix took a fortifying gulp from his cup, spilling a few drops on his mouse-grey doublet.

And for once, even Solomon Tree was lost for words.

Chapter Eight

The next day was cloudy, but the air had warmed and the snow was melting fast. Not that Lord Bonner's Men noticed the weather, for they had only one thing on their minds: the confrontation with their rivals. They gathered in a close little group on Bankside, in a lane that led away from the river. A hundred and fifty yards away stood the new Swan Theatre. A flag with the device of a swan flew above the stage roof, which was visible behind the houses.

The players were restless, for as usual they had been kept waiting by Daniel Rix. But just as they were about to give up on him, the playmaker appeared, hurrying along the street towards them. Then John Symes gave a sign, and the company turned and walked up the lane. Ben Button and Matt Fields obeyed John's instructions, and kept to the rear. In a short time they had reached the high walls of the Swan. The doors were closed, but Will Sanders tried the handle and found them unlocked. So without further ado they shoved the doors wide and marched into the theatre yard. And as they had expected, they walked into the middle of a rehearsal.

There were several people standing on the high stage, and someone in a crown and robe was declaiming a speech. As the company strode in, the man stopped and turned. His fellows did the same – and the silence that fell was so sudden, Ben thought he could hear his heart thump.

"Master Symes?" James Mostyn was the player in the king's costume, and he was shocked at seeing Lord Bonner's players walk in. There was even fear in his eyes as they came to a halt – Ben, on the edge of the group, saw it plainly. But soon the man's expression turned to one of anger.

"What do you want here?" With a sharp movement, Mostyn took the crown off and strode to the front of the stage. But John stepped forward, gesturing to Will Sanders. Will shook out the white cloth he had been carrying, and held it up.

"We want to talk," John said. "We're not here to make trouble. This kerchief will serve as our flag of truce."

There was a snort from one of the other men on the stage. Ben glanced at him and saw he was a sour-faced fellow. Indeed, now that he had chance to observe some of the Earl of Horsham's players at close quarters, he saw that their reputation as a rough lot was well deserved. There were scowls, and some of them began muttering. And now Lord Bonner's Men grew restive in their turn. The wounding of Hugh Cotton was fresh in their minds – not to mention the fire, the theft of the costumes, and the attack on Ben and Matt by the boys.

Just then, Ben felt a sharp dig in his ribs. He looked round to see Matt nodding towards the rear of the stage – and when Ben followed his gaze, he gave a start. Standing at one side, dressed as a woman-in-waiting, was none other than "Rat" Ratcliff. Then Matt gasped – and Ben stifled one of his own.

Rat was wearing a splendid lilac gown, embroidered with gold thread, that both boys recognized. It was the Lady Celia costume for *The Witch of Wandsworth* that had been made specially for Matt. And Matt would have called out, had Ben not grabbed his arm. His instincts told him that this matter should wait. With a shake of his head, Ben signalled that they should keep silent.

"Flag of truce?" James Mostyn was frowning down at John. "Why would you need such? If you've something to say, you could have spoken with me at any time!"

Mostyn's fellow players began bunching together. Instinctively, Bonner's Men did the same, and Ben and Matt both tensed. In his mind, Ben saw Rat and the other boys charging towards him, as they had three days back in the snow. Now it looked like another fight was about to break out – but this would be a far worse one.

"Stop!" John looked round angrily at his company. When they grew still, he turned back to Mostyn.

"If there's to be a tussle, I will not start it." John met the other man's eye. "You know there are matters that stand between us. Yet I don't come here to make accusations—"

"Accusations!" Mostyn glared. "I can't think what they could be, save that we're better performers than you! What do you accuse us of – stealing your audience?"

Some of Horsham's Men laughed. Whereupon

Solomon Tree, who had been standing at John's shoulder, gave a groan.

"I wouldn't accuse your comic of stealing my jokes," he called. "Since nobody laughs at them, they can't be mine. Come to think of it, I haven't heard much applause carry from the Swan to the Rose, even when the wind's right. Are you sure you've *got* an audience?"

Now it was the turn of Bonner's Men to laugh, before John Symes gestured them to be quiet. "That's enough, Master Tree," he murmured, keeping a straight face. To James Mostyn he said: "You will have heard the tidings from the Rose – for as we all know, gossip spreads on Bankside as fast as fire!"

John paused to let the words strike home. And Lord Bonner's players watched their rivals carefully. For if there had been alarm on the face of any man, they would know that at least one of them could have been involved in the fire that burned down the store-hut. Ben peered at Rat, but the other boy showed no sign that he had even noticed Ben or Matt. He gazed towards the empty galleries, and avoided looking at anyone.

"Of course we know of your troubles!" Mostyn waved a hand, as if to dismiss the matter. "Everyone does – yet what players' company hasn't suffered hardship? And thefts of costumes are not unknown—"

"What of malicious wounding?"

Gabriel Tucker pushed past Will to stand at the front of the group. Ignoring John Symes's warning look, the little man raised a finger and pointed it at James Mostyn.

"Hugh Cotton lies abed, recovering from a sword thrust that narrowly missed his heart!" he cried. "Do you know about that, too?"

There were some frightened looks on the faces of Horsham's Men. This, as the constable had said, was a hanging offence. And watching their reactions, Ben decided that none of these were behind the attack on Hugh. Indeed, they seemed shocked that anyone might suspect them. And unease showed on James Mostyn's face now, as he turned his eyes upon Gabriel.

"I know you, Master Tucker," he said. "You're a hothead – and you'll pay for your hasty words! For if you accuse us of having any part in the attack on Master Cotton, I'll swear out a warrant against you for slander! It's monstrous – and our patron will hear of it—"

"As will ours!" It was John Symes's turn to get angry. "In fact he has been sent word already, of the trials we have suffered!" Controlling himself, John turned to Gabriel and put a restraining hand on his arm, for the little player was bristling like a cockerel.

"As I've said, we came to accuse no one," John said. "But we did come to deliver a warning – and I advise you and your fellows to heed it!" And though Mostyn and the other men scowled, he seemed not to notice.

"So I say this," John went on. "If I have the smallest suspicion that you or your fellows have worked against us in any way except as players in fair competition, then it is I who will swear out the warrant, James Mostyn! And any man who sets himself at one of us, sets himself against the whole company! Do I make myself clear?"

There were more angry murmurings from Horsham's players, but a look from Mostyn was enough to silence them. Turning back to John, he seemed to collect himself before answering.

"Perfectly," he said. "So let's understand each other. We will keep to our end of Bankside, at the Swan. You keep to yours, at the Rose. The stairs where we take a boat shall be neutral ground, as are the streets. But hear this..." Mostyn pointed a warning finger at John. "If you dare to come boldly into our theatre again as you have, throwing out hints, if not accusations, then you will pay!"

John did not answer. And now the confrontation was over. Without a word, Mostyn turned and walked away towards the tiring-room door. His fellows followed, after throwing a few threatening looks at Lord Bonner's Men. But there would be no fight. With some relief, but with scores still unsettled, Bonner's Men turned to leave the theatre yard. And only then, at the last moment, did Daniel Rix speak up.

Along with his fellows, Ben had almost forgotten that the playmaker was there. They looked round as Rix cleared his throat, then addressed Solomon.

"I'm somewhat dismayed by what you said, Master Tree," he murmured. "Suggesting their comic doesn't get any laughs, I mean..." He sighed. "You see, I wrote his jokes."

It was midday, when the players stopped rehearsal to take their dinner, before Ben could speak to John Symes about the Lady Celia costume. He and Matt soon realized that none of the other players had noticed it during the confrontation at the Swan. Since then, the two boys had talked privately in the tiring room. Now they walked up to John, who was sitting on a bench at one side of the stage, and told him their news.

"But this changes everything!" John said sharply. "Why did you not speak up before? Now it looks as if Horsham's Men are indeed the thieves!"

"We saw one costume," Ben said. "It doesn't mean they took them all...or indeed that the others know where Rat got the Lady Celia gown." He looked at Matt.

"I know Ratcliff, Master John," Matt said. "He's a nasty piece of work – he could be the thief, for he's done worse." He glanced at Ben, who nodded.

"We need proof," Ben said. "So we...well, I thought..."

He broke off, and John began to understand. Gazing at his prentice, he said: "I smell a conspiracy. Could it be that you've formed one of your *plans*?"

"Well, not quite – it's just a feeling," Ben answered. "But if you'd care to hear it..."

Someone had once called Ben *the ferret*, after his skill at ferreting things out. And sometimes his sharp eyes indeed seemed to spot things that others missed. Now, thinking hard on all that had happened, he knew he was on a trail of some sort, and was keen to follow the scent. Eagerly he spoke of it to John Symes – and to his relief Matt kept quiet. After some doubts, John agreed – though reluctantly, and with a strong warning.

"Very well – I'll give you two days to poke about, and no more," he said. "I'm sure my message will have reached Lord Bonner at his country house by now. He'll come to London soon in any case, for the Christmas Revels – and when he arrives, he will want explanations." John fixed them both with a grave look. "So I'm trusting you to keep your word. Discover what you can, and if it amounts to hard evidence we can lay it before the constable, and have him charge Horsham's Men with theft. But mark what I said: you must stay clear of any trouble."

He sighed, and Ben saw the strain his master was under. Not only was he worried about the money they were losing while the Rose remained closed, but he had also taken on Hugh Cotton's difficult role of Adam. He and Will Sanders had been poring over the play with Daniel Rix, working out who should take over which parts. At least Ben's and Matt's roles were unchanged; no one else could take theirs.

And so it was settled, and the two of them left John alone. They went out of the Rose, into the lane. Then they walked some distance before stopping beside one of the large ponds – the Pike Garden, it was called, where the huge fish were reared for eating. There they sat down on a log, whereupon Matt spoke up in a voice of consternation.

"How on earth did I let you talk me into this, Buttonhead?"

"I haven't talked you into anything yet," Ben answered.

"Haven't you?" Matt retorted. "Well hear this: spotting the stolen costume is one thing – but how do you mean to prove Rat took it? Wait for him by the stairs and ask him? *Excuse me, Rat, but are you a thief? And how would you like to be hanged?*"

"That wasn't what I had in mind," Ben told him.

When Matt said nothing, he went on: "We're players, aren't we? So we must use our imagination. We can disguise ourselves, for a start."

"Disguise ourselves as what?" Matt demanded.

Ben did not answer right away. The idea that had been forming back at the theatre was now clear in his mind. And he couldn't resist a smile as he turned to Matt and began to lay out the plan.

Matt listened, and his frown deepened until he was glowering into the dark waters of the pike pond. At last he raised his head and met Ben's eye with a look of disbelief.

"But half of London has seen Bonner's Men perform!" he exclaimed. "People know what we look like – so what sort of disguise do you mean? Are you going to go in your witch's garb?"

Ben grinned at him. "It's best we dress as women," he said. "But I've a better idea. You can play yourself – I'll play your mother."

Matt merely stared at him, as if he had lost his senses.

Chapter Nine

The first part of the plan was the hardest.

The afternoon waned, and Lord Bonner's Men had gone their separate ways. Only John Symes and Daniel Rix lingered at the Rose, sitting by candlelight to work on the parts for *The Witch of Wandsworth*. So it was easy enough for Ben and Matt to slip away for a while. Dusk was falling as the two boys hurried along Bankside to the lane that led to the Swan Theatre. There they concealed themselves in a narrow alley between two tumbledown houses, and waited.

Luckily they had not long to wait. A few minutes later a group of men came past talking and headed for the Falcon Stairs. Ben and Matt held their breath as they recognized several of Horsham's players, including James Mostyn. But disappointment flooded over Ben, for he saw that among them were two boys: Rat, and the long-haired one called Gaddy – the one who had attacked Ben, before coming off worst in the tussle.

None of the group saw him or Matt. As they walked by, their voices fading, Ben felt a tug at his sleeve.

"I know him now," Matt breathed. "His name's Tom Gadd."

"We must get hold of one of them," Ben whispered impatiently. "We need to get him away from his fellows…"

There was a sound of footsteps, and both of them tensed: someone else was coming down the lane. They ducked low, and peered out of their hiding place to see a slight figure walking quickly, as if to catch up with the others. And Ben stiffened, for he knew who it was: the skinny boy who had pinned him while Gaddy struck him – and whom Ben had sent away howling.

He was abreast of them, then he was past them.

Like the others, he did not know he was being watched. Ben was about to spring – but before he knew what was happening, Matt had leaped out into the lane, grabbed the boy from behind and dragged him backwards into the alley. He clamped one hand over the fellow's mouth, or no doubt he would have howled as he had done the other night. Instead, recognizing his captors at once, the boy began to struggle like an eel. But Ben and Matt soon overpowered him, and thrust him to the ground. There he sat, his back against a wall, gazing at them in fear. Only then did Matt take his hand from the boy's mouth. Then he dropped to one knee, facing him.

"Don't hurt me! I'm not the one you want!" The boy wet his lips nervously. "It was Rat's notion," he said hoarsely. "He wanted to stalk you. I didn't want to, but he—"

"Stop your mouth," Matt said in a steely voice, and at once the skinny boy fell silent. Even Ben was surprised at Matt's tone. He sounded like someone who was well and truly in charge.

"What's your name?" Matt asked.

"Laney," came the answer. "Richard Laney..."

"Well, Master Richard..." Matt leaned close, so that the boy flinched. "We've got a few questions, and you're going to supply the answers. But if you lie, I'll know it – and I'll make you regret it." Matt paused to let his words sink in. "Now, are you going to help us or not?"

Richard Laney nodded quickly.

"Good." Matt glanced briefly at Ben, then asked: "Where did your friend Rat get that gown? The one trimmed with gold?"

"Is that all you want to know?" the other asked in surprise.

"Just answer me," Matt said.

"Our tiring-man bought it for him," Laney said with a shrug. "He buys all our costumes."

"Bought it where?" Matt kept his eyes on the other's face.

"A fripperer's stall, in Houndsditch," came the answer. Then Laney gasped. "It was yours, wasn't it?" he cried. "One of those that got stolen…"

But Matt silenced him with a glare. "This fripperer," he snapped. "What's his name?"

Laney blinked. "It's her, not him," he replied. "The company buys a lot of hand-me-downs from her. She's called Agnes Hart."

Matt looked at Ben, for Laney's words had the ring of truth to them. Fripperers were dealers in second-hand clothes – and it was indeed possible that whoever stole their costumes could have sold them for ready money.

Taking his turn now, Ben fixed his gaze upon the boy.

"What else has your company bought?" he asked. "Do you know about a silver-lace doublet, or a saffron suit?"

"No." Laney shook his head vigorously. "I swear I don't. Since the summer, we buy cheap as we can." A bitter look came over his face. "Our patron isn't so rich as your Lord Bonner," he muttered. "And he don't mollycoddle us, passing on his fine clothes."

But Ben had another thought. Leaning closer to Master Laney, he asked: "Who set the store-hut on fire?"

Laney gulped, suddenly afraid. "I don't know!" he cried. "You've got to believe me—"

"That's where you're wrong," Matt Fields said. And at a glance from him, Ben sat back to let his companion do the talking.

"I don't have to believe you, Master Richard," Matt went on, making the boy flinch. "And I say that even if you didn't set the hut ablaze, likely you know who did."

But Laney merely shook his head.

"I'm getting impatient," Matt said. And when still

no answer followed, his hand shot out to grab the skinny fellow by the throat. Ben winced, remembering what that felt like.

"Don't!" Laney grabbed hold of Matt's wrist and began to struggle, but Matt was too strong. "I want a name," he said. "And if you were thinking of making one up, think again!"

Laney began to shake. He was plainly scared out of his wits.

"I don't know who did it," he whispered. "I swear it!"

Ben gave a sigh of disappointment. And for a brief moment, Matt let go of Richard Laney – which was all their captive needed. With lightning speed, the boy tore himself from Matt's grasp, rolled away and scrambled to his feet. Ben darted forward to grab him, but Matt gripped his arm.

"Let him go," he said. "He's told us all he can."

They had one name, at least: Agnes Hart.

She was the fripperer in Houndsditch who had sold Horsham's Men the stolen costume. And she was the reason Ben Button was up early the next morning, before even John was dressed. Alice Symes came down the stairs to find him unbolting the front door carefully, trying not to wake anyone. The old hound Brutus sat nearby, watching him with a puzzled look. There was a bundle under Ben's arm – and seeing Alice's expression, he realized that he must look suspicious.

"I've got something to do before I go to the theatre," he said. "Please tell John I'll be there as soon as I can."

Alice frowned. "What about your breakfast?"

But Ben had already pulled the door open. And before she could speak again, he was gone.

He met Matt on the corner of Houndsditch near the Dolphin Inn, where three mornings ago he had watched a snowball fight. It was chilly and damp, but already London was astir. The two boys ducked into an alley beside the inn, where Ben could change into his costume while Matt kept watch. When he was ready, he emerged into the street – whereupon Matt broke into a grin.

"Well, I'll give you credit, Buttonhead. You don't look like my mother, but you'd pass for someone her age all right."

Ben was wearing an old russet-coloured gown of Alice's, with the hem pinned up. Over it he wore a plain white apron. He carried a basket, and on his head was a straw hat, the sort countrywomen wore when they came to market. He had also reddened his cheeks, and whitened his eyebrows with flour. With the grey wig that poked from under his hat, he looked like a short, middle-aged matron out to do her shopping. And as such a woman might, she had brought her son along to carry her parcels. Seeing Master Fields's smirk, Ben couldn't resist the chance to get his own back.

"Take my arm, Matthew, and hurry up!" he snapped in a high, crotchety voice. "We haven't got all day!"

There were folk on the streets now, coming out of Bishopsgate. Most turned into Houndsditch, from where street sellers' cries could be heard. So with a wry look, Matt took Ben's arm, and the pair of them moved off among the other women. To Ben's satisfaction, nobody gave them a second glance.

The street was lined with stalls. Clothes of every kind could be bought here – some of good quality, some little better than rags. Poor folk in search of winter attire mixed with better-off housewives looking for bargains. Some had a servant with them to carry their goods. Leaning on Matt's arm, Ben made his way along the row. At the first few stalls, they stopped to look at gowns and skirts, hats and cloaks, sometimes annoying the stallholders, who could tell that they were not buying. Once or twice they were told roughly to move on. Finally Matt bent low, and spoke in Ben's ear.

"I'm getting tired of this," he whispered. "Why don't we ask for Agnes Hart and be done with it?"

But Ben slapped his hand. "Hold your tongue, young man!" he scolded. "We'll go when I'm ready, and not before!"

One or two folk laughed, whereupon Matt tightened his grip on Ben's arm. "I won't forget this, Buttonhead," he muttered.

They were passing in front of a stall piled with brightly coloured clothes: men's doublets and breeches, shirts and hose. There was also a cloak with a red silk lining...and then Ben stopped in his tracks. Matt looked round and followed his gaze, before he too stiffened. For there was another cloak, that both of them recognized at once.

It was of black velvet, edged with silver – and it had belonged to Lord Bonner's Men.

With a sharp breath, Ben moved closer to the stall and reached for the cloak – whereupon a squeaky voice startled him.

"'Tis but five shillings, goodwife! A true bargain!"

Ben peered about, but saw no one. Then he realized that the voice came from behind a pile of clothes. As he and Matt watched, a face appeared to one side of it: that of a tiny, apple-cheeked woman, barely four-feet high. Her head and shoulders just cleared the top of her stall, and she was smiling broadly.

"The black and silver, mistress – is it for your husband? It would make a fine gift!"

Ben and Matt exchanged glances. And quickly Ben spoke up.

"Are you Mistress Hart?" he asked.

"I am," the little woman answered. "And whatever ye lack, I have it! No customer leaves Agnes Hart unsatisfied. I should have a sign done out in Latin to say it, like playmakers do in their books!"

Ben smiled. "Do you have many dealings with the theatre folk?" he asked.

Agnes Hart laughed cheerfully. "I do, mistress," she said. "And you've a sharp eye, for that very cloak you fancy was bought off a player, only two days back!"

Ben nodded. "That's small surprise to me," he said, struggling to keep his matron's voice. "My son Matthew here's a player himself, with a famous company. Do you not recognize him?"

Matt gulped, then turned it into a cough. He flinched as Mistress Hart turned her bright blue eyes upon him.

"Well, it could be that I do know the face," she said. "Would the young master be one of the Lord Chamberlain's, out at Shoreditch? And isn't that a turnabout – for I believe 'twas one of your own company that sold me this very cloak!"

She chuckled, but it was Ben's turn to gulp. "The Lord Chamberlain's Men?" He glanced at Matt. "Then likely we know the fellow... Do you recall his name?"

But Mistress Hart was busy now, gathering up the black velvet cloak. Expertly she let the fine material run across her arm like water. "I do not, mistress," she replied absently. "Now, what think you? Is five shillings not a paltry sum for such a garment? Indeed, I'm a fool to let it go so cheap!" She shrugged, then gave another chuckle. "But your son's a player you say, so I'll be generous. Four shillings, and it's yours!"

Ben reached out to touch the velvet. "It's very fine," he said. Keeping a casual tone, he asked: "Tell me, the one who sold it to you – the Chamberlain's man. Was he a tall, handsome fellow with a neat beard? For if so, he's a friend of ours..."

Agnes Hart's smile faded. "No, goodwife, I fear 'twas not your friend." She shook her head. "And I would be hard pressed to describe that red-haired, buck-toothed fellow as handsome! More like a rabbit in a ginger wig, if you ask me!"

She gave a shout of laughter. But the cloak slipped from Ben's hand, and he stepped back. Beside him, Matt Fields let out a gasp. Forgetting Agnes Hart, the two of them turned to each other in dismay, the same name on both their lips.

Tom the Teeth!

Chapter Ten

That morning's rehearsal was a tense affair for
Ben and Matt. They had agreed to keep their
discovery to themselves until they could speak to
John alone, but both were thinking about one of the
players who was not present. John Symes's hope was
that the theatre could soon reopen, whereupon he
would recall the hired men. In the meantime, the
regular members rehearsed new songs, and tried not
to think too much about the Christmas Revels.

Ben did not know Tom the Teeth well. He knew he
was a talented player, who could take a lot of roles.

Like his friend Simon Jewell, he lived on Bankside. He had been with many acting companies – even the Lord Chamberlain's Men, Ben seemed to remember. Perhaps that was why Tom had been bold enough to call himself one of them when he sold Agnes Hart the stolen cloak.

The fact that there had been a thief in the company after all weighed heavily upon Ben. He remembered the shocked look on all their faces – including Tom the Teeth's – when Will discovered that the first costume was missing. Now, there was no doubt that the others, or at least the Lady Celia costume, had also been stolen and sold to Mistress Hart. Ben and Matt had been so taken aback by their discovery, they did not think to ask her about the lilac gown that was now being worn by Rat Ratcliff. What seemed important was that they tell John their tale, at the first opportunity.

They rehearsed all morning, until John at last called a halt. The company broke up, talking among themselves as they left the stage. There had been no word from their patron, Lord Bonner. John had also sent messages to Alderman Gilbert, without receiving any reply. But though his cares were great, when Ben and Matt approached him he led them into the tiring room and sat them down. Here the boys wasted no time in breaking their news. But instead of being shocked, John looked almost as if he had expected such a discovery.

"You suspected there was a traitor," he said to Ben. "And when I thought more upon it, I realized how hard it would be for an outsider to get into the costume store. Yet I'm truly sorry it turns out to be Tom Towne, for I like the man." He gave a heavy sigh. "And I never thought him capable of this!"

"He lives nearby, and he knows Bankside," Matt put in. "Could it not be he who started the fire as well?"

John looked uncomfortable, and did not answer. Ben too found it hard to believe that Tom the Teeth would do such. If the theatre had burned down, he would have lost his livelihood along with everyone else. And he had seemed as upset as the others when Alderman Gilbert had walked in two days before and closed down the Rose.

"Do you have any other evidence of the theft?" John asked suddenly. "Apart from the word of the fripperer?"

Ben shook his head. "Not really. And we couldn't buy the cloak back, since we didn't have four shillings between us."

"No matter...I'll send someone to buy it," John said. He stood up and clapped Ben on the shoulder.

"You've done well. And I think we've enough reason to confront Master Towne. Even if that cloak were worth only four shillings, stealing it would be a felony. And even if it were the man's first offence, he would find himself branded as a thief. Yet it's still my hope that he'll make a full confession!"

But Tom the Teeth never made the confession. And that gloomy Wednesday afternoon brought further discoveries that only deepened the mystery.

Neither Ben nor Matt were allowed to go with John to Tom's lodgings. Instead, Micklewright the constable accompanied him, along with Solomon Tree and Gabriel Tucker. The two prentices had no choice but to wait with Will Sanders at the Rose. It was dark before John returned, and Will had lit the brazier in the theatre yard. There the three of them stood warming themselves, until John at last came in. He was alone – and his words took them by surprise.

"Tom the Teeth's disappeared," he said. "His clothes are still at his lodging house, but no one there has seen him for two days."

Will Sanders grunted. "He's done a flit," he said. "That proves he's the thief!"

"It looks that way," John admitted. "And now we can't prove anything. What's more, it means Horsham's Men may be innocent, after all."

Ben was quiet. Despite all they had learned, he still believed that one or more of Horsham's company were involved in the business. Though in what way, he did not know.

"Well, I've had enough for one day," John said in a tired voice. "Let's go home, and see what tomorrow brings."

Ben and Matt went to get their belongings, while Will brought a pail of water and doused the brazier. It was still steaming as they walked to the entrance. They were almost at the doors, when there came a sound that startled all of them: a loud creak.

John Symes turned sharply. Will stopped, then in an instant he was hurrying towards the lower seating gallery.

"Bring a light!" he cried. "There's something wrong!"

John got out his tinderbox and struck a flame, while Ben and Matt followed Will to the bottom step of the gallery. He stopped before one of the posts that held up the balcony above. They were of stout and solid oak. Will dropped to one knee, then turned to take the light John Symes handed him. Holding the flame close to the post he examined it carefully. Then he gave a shout.

"It's been sawn through – almost halfway!"

John kneeled beside Will. Ben and Matt bent to look – and they too saw the deep cut that had been made near the base of the post. As everyone stared, there was another creak from the beam overhead.

Will sat back. "You know what this means?" he asked John in a shaky voice. "If we'd given a performance..."

"I see it!" John's face was pale in the dim light. Ben and Matt exchanged glances – they too understood what a disaster the sawn pillar would have caused. If the theatre had been packed, as it was for the opening of *The Witch of Wandsworth*, a whole gallery full of people would likely have collapsed onto those below. There would not merely have been injuries, there would have been deaths too.

Will ran his hand around the boards at the bottom of the post, then examined his palm. "Fresh sawdust," he muttered. "Whoever did this, did it within the last day or two, when there was no one here..." He gave a start. "Like yesterday, while we were all at the Swan arguing with Horsham's lot!"

John nodded grimly. "If that's so, then we can't accuse them of this," he said. "For they had no inkling we were coming!" He put a hand to his brow, and his voice dropped almost to a whisper. "This is the most evil thing that's happened to us," he said.

"Even worse than the attack upon Hugh. For whoever did it meant to cause mayhem on a grand scale – and he cared not who his victims were!"

The others were silent, until Ben spoke up.

"Surely Tom the Teeth wouldn't do this," he said quietly. "Would he?

"He could have slipped in while we weren't here," Will began. Then he fell silent, for John was shaking his head.

"I can't believe he would be party to such an evil deed, either," he said. "Nor has he been seen for days." He got heavily to his feet. After a moment, Will stood up too, and handed back his tinderbox.

"I'll get a carpenter here tomorrow," John said as he snuffed the flame out. "We'll have to check every timber – there may be others damaged..." He sighed. "If there were any doubts before, there can be none now. For somebody – if not one of Horsham's, then someone else – is determined to ruin Lord Bonner's Men. I'm not sure why – but I know one thing: he doesn't care how he does it!"

"There's one thing we can do," Will said. "We can keep a watch on the Rose at all times. I'll sleep here tonight, in the tiring room. And I'll be well armed!"

"Then I know the theatre will be in safe hands," John said, with an approving glance at Will. He drew a deep breath, and looked at each of them. "Tomorrow I'm going to see Alderman Gilbert," he added. "Since he seems to think he's the most important man hereabouts, let him do something about the sabotage!"

So it was agreed that from that night on, Will Sanders would act as nightwatchman at the Rose. Though to Ben it seemed unlikely that anyone would try to get in again. For the damage had been done: even if the theatre reopened, Lord Bonner's Men could not perform, or at least not until the building was made safe.

A gloom hung over the company the next day. They had all heard the news, and it was not only Solomon Tree who was glum-faced. It seemed now as if some force were set against them – but one they could not see. John's determination to speak with Alderman Gilbert did not cheer them much. The alderman had wanted the theatre closed from the start – now it was beginning to look as if it would not reopen this side of Christmas.

John left at midday. Will Sanders had gone to Houndsditch to get the stolen cloak back from Agnes Hart, while Solomon and Gabriel practised a few songs in half-hearted fashion. So, finding themselves at a loose end, Ben and Matt went out into Maiden Lane. It was a sunny day, and both boys were restless. Ben had woken up early, his mind busy with recent events. He wanted to talk things over, but, seeing Matt was in one of his sullen moods, he decided against it. And a short time later, scarcely knowing why, Ben found himself walking alone down to the riverside.

There were plenty of people about. His curiosity getting the better of him, Ben wandered past taverns and alehouses, some of them noisy, others oddly quiet. Several buildings looked forbidding to him, and he gave them a wide berth. He guessed that they were dicing-houses and bowl-alleys, where men went to gamble. Though those who came out seldom looked very happy, he thought. Since everyone knew that cheating was common in such places, he wondered why they were so busy.

After an hour or so he was bored, and ready to head back to the Rose. He was at the western end of Bankside, above the Falcon Stairs. There seemed to be a lot of boats on the water, and several were jostling for space by the jetty. Then from behind him a trumpet rang out – a loud blast that carried over the rooftops. At once he knew where it came from: the Swan Theatre. The Earl of Horsham's Men were about to start their performance. Already people were clambering from their boats and hurrying up the stairs, while others were crowding into the lane. Only now did he remember that he was in the territory of the enemy company.

Then Ben had an idea: he would go to the play.

As a player he had appeared on stage dozens of times – yet he never went to a theatre the way most people did, as one of the audience. Surely no one would notice him? So a few minutes later he was paying his penny to the gate-holder at the Swan, and joining the crowds as they flocked into the yard.

The trumpet had sounded for a second time while he queued outside. At the third sounding, the crowd grew excited. Ben was excited too – even if he were on dangerous ground. He pushed that thought away: now, he was curious to see Horsham's company act. Then he could judge for himself whether they were any good or not.

There was a loud bang on a drum, and from the gallery above the stage, musicians struck up a lively opening. The tiring-room doors flew open and several brightly dressed players emerged. "*The Battle of Alcazar!*" a voice cried, and a roar went up from the crowd. Even Ben found his heart lift: the play had begun!

But as it turned out, the opening of *The Battle of Alcazar* was all he was going to see.

He was standing to the left of the stage, pressed between folk on all sides: men and women, most of humble station, who had paid their hard-earned pennies and were eager for entertainment. Among them moved hawkers selling bottles of ale, and others with baskets of apples or hazelnuts. The noise was great from the galleries above and around him, and in the yard there was laughter and chatter on every side. Outside, it was a winter's day, but in here the heat from packed bodies turned the theatre into a kitchen. Whereupon Ben was suddenly uneasy: he remembered that there were some who worked the crowds for different purposes. Quickly he put his hand to his belt, to make sure his purse was safe. There were only a few pennies in it, but to him that was a lot.

The purse was there. Relaxing, he turned his attention back to the stage. Now he saw James Mostyn, dressed as the King of Portugal, walk out to a scattering of applause. There were others making their entrances too – Ben tensed, expecting to see Rat at any moment. His glance strayed towards several fashionable gentlemen who were taking their seats on the edge of the stage. He sighed – sometimes he had to fetch stools for such customers, who were there to be seen by their friends rather than to watch the play. He looked past them...and his heart gave a jolt.

There was no mistaking the bright red hair. And almost before he knew it, Ben was pushing through the crowd. Being small and nimble, it did not take him long to work his way towards the man he had seen. Then, when the fellow happened to glance to one side, Ben froze: he was not mistaken.

But it was not the sight of Tom the Teeth that had startled him, so much as the realization of what he was up to. Even as Ben struggled to get closer, he saw the small knife in the man's palm. No one else noticed – they were all intent upon the action on stage. But Ben watched, heart in mouth, as Tom the Teeth cut the purse from the belt of a man in front of him – so swiftly and so skilfully that the victim felt nothing. Nor did anyone else see what had happened.

Ben shouted, but no one paid him any mind – and in any case he was too late. For, by instinct, Tom the Teeth swung round and looked straight at him. His eyes widened – and in an instant he had dived into the crowd.

Chapter Eleven

The crush of people reached almost to the doors of the Swan. There the gate-holder stood, taking money from latecomers who were hurrying in. But Tom the Teeth did not slow his pace. He simply shoved two or three men roughly aside, ignoring their protests, and forced himself through the half-open doors. Then he was gone.

But Ben was close behind. He slipped easily between the doors, and was soon outside the theatre. The noise of the crowd faded quickly. Once in the open, he peered ahead – and saw the red-haired figure, running across the fields towards Lambeth Marsh. Without stopping to think of the consequences, he chased after him.

Ben had always been swift on his feet. Tom the Teeth, he soon realized, was not nearly as quick. In less than a minute Ben was closing on him, leaping over logs and other obstacles as he did. Then he saw the drainage ditch, right across Tom the Teeth's path. Tom saw it too and speeded up, preparing to jump over it. And that was Tom's mistake: for though with a great bound he managed to clear the ditch, he landed clumsily on the other side, and fell over. He got up quickly, but his right foot crumpled under him. And with a cry of pain, Tom sat down heavily on the ground. This time he did not get up.

Ben took a run, jumped the ditch and landed lightly, bending his knees. Then he stood up, out of breath, and gazed down at the man who, only a few days ago, had been one of his fellow players. Now he looked like a fugitive – and Ben was the one who had caught him. He could hardly believe what had happened.

"Well, Master Button – are you content?" Tom the Teeth spoke harshly, as he too struggled to get his breath back. "I've twisted an ankle! So if you're set on fetching an officer of the law, you'd best do it – for you won't get a better chance than this!"

At first Ben was lost for words. Then a dozen questions crowded into his mind. But before he could open his mouth, the other spoke again.

"Why were you following me?" Tom demanded. "Who sent you?"

"No one sent me," Ben answered. "I just happened to go to the theatre."

Tom the Teeth stared, but said nothing. Now that Ben was close to him, he saw the sorry state the man was in. His clothes were dirty, his hair and beard untidy. He looked like someone who had been in hiding – and suddenly, the fight seemed to go out of him. His expression changed, and he gazed up at Ben with a look of desperation.

"Well, what will you do?" he asked. "For if I'm caught this time, I'll hang for sure! Is that what you want?"

"Of course it isn't," Ben replied.

"Then will you show mercy?" Without waiting for an answer, Tom got up slowly, wincing when he put his right foot down. But this time he stayed upright.

Ben found himself in a quandary. He had seen Tom the Teeth steal a purse, and knew that he should tell a constable. But, assuming the man was telling the truth, he would be hanged...

He took a deep breath and asked: "Why did you

steal the costumes from the tiring room?"

"I had no choice," Tom said, after a moment. "It was do as I was ordered, or..." He broke off with a sigh, and looked away.

"Ordered?" Ben echoed. "By whom?"

But there was no answer from Tom. And now Ben felt angry. He thought of all the troubles Lord Bonner's Men had had since they came to Bankside, and realized that this man had been the cause of them – or at least, of some of them.

"The fire, in the hut," he said. "Did you—"

"No!" Tom the Teeth shook his head. "I swear it wasn't me."

"Then who was it?" Ben demanded.

"Don't ask me," Tom said, with a grim expression. "For you've no inkling of the people you're dealing with!"

"Haven't I?" Ben countered. "After what happened to Hugh? You were only feet away from him...you saw for yourself—"

"Enough!" Tom took a step, then grunted with pain. He gazed about, as if to make sure there was no one within earshot. Then he faced Ben – and there was no mistaking the fear in his eyes.

"I saw," he muttered. "And if I could have done anything to stop it, I—"

"I don't believe you," Ben said.

Tom the Teeth lowered his eyes. He appeared so forlorn, Ben almost pitied him. Then an idea struck him, which drove all such thoughts from his mind.

"You know who he is, don't you?" he said quietly. "The fellow who stabbed Hugh."

Tom made no reply, but his expression was enough. And suddenly, Ben understood. "Of course you know!" he went on. "For that was how he got into the tiring room unnoticed, wasn't it? You helped him! You had a costume ready for him…"

"I've told you, I had no choice!" Tom the Teeth almost spat the words. Now he grew desperate. His hand even went to his belt, to the dagger in its sheath. Then he stopped himself, and dropped his arm. To Ben's dismay, a sob came from the man's throat.

"Ask no more, Master Button…" Tom shook his head mournfully. "One day, when you're older, you will understand the sort of troubles a man can bring upon himself."

He paused, then went on: "We all have weaknesses. Mine is for dice and cards. I owed money, to men who would squeeze me hard to make me pay. And too late, I found another man had bought up all my debts. It was he…"

Again Tom broke off, but Ben had stopped listening. He was thinking of Hugh, lying abed with his wounds, and of John and the others, and how worried they had been.

"You've been the cause of our troubles," he said angrily. "You were the traitor inside Lord Bonner's Men all along, bent on ruining us—"

"No!" Tom the Teeth snapped. "I'm but a hired man – a servant! I'm not your enemy—"

"Then who is?" Ben threw back. "We know Mostyn and his fellows want us out of Bankside, but John doesn't believe they would stoop to murder—"

"And he's right!" Tom's tone was harsh. He looked about again, and it seemed to Ben that he was weighing up what to do. Finally he drew a sleeve across his face, and said: "If I give you a name, will you let me walk away?"

Ben hesitated. He was torn between his anger and a burning curiosity to know who was behind the things that had happened. And what was more, though he no longer felt much pity for Tom the Teeth, he did not want to see the man go to the gallows. Seeing Ben struggle with his feelings, Tom spoke again.

"A half-hour is all I ask, young master," he said. "A half-hour to get away. Then you can go to John Symes and tell him all, as you're bound to do. I'd not blame you if you refused, for I'm a worthless fellow..." He sighed again. "You know little of me," he went on. "But it matters not. I'll be gone from London, and take my chances on the road. It's where I came from."

Ben saw again the desperation in the man's eyes. He was a weak and troubled fellow, but not a wicked one. With a heavy heart, Ben made his decision.

"Give me the purse you took at the Swan," he said. "Then tell me the name."

Tom the Teeth hesitated. Then he reached inside his doublet, pulled out the purse and tossed it to Ben. As Ben caught it, Tom leaned closer to him.

"It's Garth," he said. "Samuel Garth." He sniffed, and wiped his nose again. "And if you find aught else amiss, you may bet your last farthing he was behind that too!"

Ben started, remembering the post that was almost sawn through. He felt a chill down his back as he thought of the things Samuel Garth had done.

"But why?" he asked. "Who is this man, and why is he trying to ruin us?"

Tom shrugged, but would not answer.

"Then, do you know where he can be found?" Ben persisted.

But Tom was shaking his head. "That's all I'll tell you," he muttered. Then he added: "And don't fret – it's not a false name. If you'll take the word of a thief upon that."

Somehow, Ben knew the man had told the truth. After a moment, he managed a nod. Deliberately he turned round, and began walking alongside the ditch. He did not look back, even when he found a plank bridge and crossed over it. Then, after he had walked for fifty yards or so, he stopped and turned.

Tom the Teeth had disappeared. And he was never seen again.

His thoughts buzzing about like bees, Ben went back to the Swan. The crowd inside sounded excited, but he did not go in. Instead he stopped before the gate-holder, and held up the purse Tom had thrown him.

"I found this in the lane, master," he said. "Someone must have dropped it."

The gate-holder was a fat man with a black beard. When he looked down, his eyes almost popped out of his head.

"By the heavens!" he exclaimed. "I've worked theatres for years, but I've never known anyone return a purse before. You're an honest lad, aren't you?"

Ben shrugged and handed the purse over. Then, with a heavy heart, he turned to go. For some reason, he did not feel as if he had been honest at all.

When he arrived back at the Rose, he found John Symes waiting for him. As soon as he saw Ben, John hurried towards him, a look of anger mixed with relief on his face.

"Where have you been?" he demanded. Then, seeing Ben's expression, he frowned. "What's happened?"

Ben took a deep breath, and told him.

By the time he had finished his tale, the whole company was standing around Ben. Will Sanders was back from Mistress Hart's, having bought back the stolen cloak. Solomon and Gabriel were there too, along with Matt. They listened in silence while Ben recounted all that Tom the Teeth had told him. But they stirred when he spoke the name of the man who had tried to kill Hugh Cotton.

"Garth?" Will grunted. "The name means nothing. Has anyone heard of him?"

The others shook their heads – all except Matt, who gave a start. He recovered quickly, and no one noticed except Ben. He caught Matt's eye, and Matt looked away. But not before Ben had seen his discomfort.

"Well, it's something to go on," John was saying.

"I'll speak to Micklewright..." He sighed. "He's our only hope," he went on. "Alderman Gilbert has refused to help in any way. He wants us gone, and that's the end of it."

Gabriel's moustache was twitching. "Then we'll do without him!" he cried. "We can start our own manhunt for this villain Garth!"

"What, search all of London?" Solomon Tree put in. "A fellow like that would go to ground, in some thieves' hideaway. You won't find him in a month of Sundays."

"Solomon's right," Will said. "If the rogue's clever enough to get into the tiring room under our noses, and then make his escape like he did, he's too clever to get himself caught that easily."

"At least we know who he is, thanks to our prentice," John said. "Though why the man did what he did remains a mystery." His brow furrowed. "Perhaps the constable knows of him."

Ben felt relieved. He was still not sure whether he had done the right thing, letting Tom the Teeth walk away. But now John seemed to guess what was in his thoughts.

"You did what you had to," he said, with a kindly look. "And whatever Tom did, I wouldn't see him hang, either."

He glanced round at the others. "The afternoon's waning," he said, "and I should go straight to Micklewright." He turned to Ben. "Do you want to come along, or wait here for me?"

Ben had been looking at Matt Fields, who still refused to meet his eye. Now he turned to John.

"I'll wait," he answered. "If Matt will wait with me."

"Very well..." John turned to Matt. "You and Ben stay until my return."

Within a few minutes he had left the theatre with Solomon and Gabriel. Will lit the brazier and went off to the tiring room, leaving the two prentices alone in the yard. The moment he was gone, Ben turned to Matt.

"You're hiding something," he said.

Matt made no reply, but he still looked uncomfortable.

Ben grabbed him by the collar of his jerkin. "I saw you, when Samuel Garth's name was mentioned," he went on angrily. "You looked as guilty as Tom the Teeth did—"

"Let go of me, Buttonhead!" Matt grabbed Ben's wrist, and tore his hand away.

But Ben was not about to give up. "You know who he is, don't you?" he cried. "I know you do! If you won't tell me, I'll run after John and fetch him back—"

"All right!" With a savage movement Matt thrust Ben away. Then he looked him in the eye, and said: "Samuel Garth was in prison with my father! Now – does that satisfy you?"

Chapter Twelve

*B*en stood beside the brazier and listened to Matt's tale. And as it unfolded, he realized how little he had known about his fellow boy actor. It was a story of hardship, the like of which he had never heard before.

Matt's father, James, had been an unlucky man – even a foolish man – but not a bad one. When he had fallen ill and been unable to work at his trade as a joiner, his guild had helped him with money, as they would help any of their members. But then James Fields had begun drinking heavily. While Matt's mother had struggled to bring up Matt and his sister, his father had fallen deeper into debt. Finally, he had gone to prison.

"He could yet have saved himself, if he'd had the strength." Matt spoke quietly, staring into the flames. "My mother raised all the money she could to pay off his debts…she got him out of the debtors' prison. But he was weakened by drink, and then he fell sick again, and he stole some money. That's how he ended up behind bars for the last time."

He turned to Ben with a bitter look. "There's no pity in jail for a man who has lost his foothold," he said. "Now you know why I said the Clink is the worst prison there is. That's where my father died!"

Ben was quiet. He no longer felt angry. Indeed, after hearing Matt's story, he felt sorry for him. Finally he spoke up.

"You've kept this secret from the company," he said. "Was it because—"

"I keep it secret because I'm ashamed!" Matt broke in. "You're the only one who knows." He looked away. "Now I suppose you'll tell John."

Ben hesitated. "Do you know where Garth lives?" he asked.

Matt gave a snort. "Lives?" he echoed. "Men like him don't live anywhere! They move about, try to stay ahead of the law..." He shook his head. "After what he did, he'll be lying very low, you can count on that."

Then, seeing the look on Ben's face, Matt grew wary. "Hold on a minute, Buttonhead," he muttered. "If you're dreaming up one of your plans, I'm having no part in it!"

"Then the least you can do is tell John what you know," Ben said. "After all that's happened...the fire, and Hugh nearly killed—"

"I know!" Matt shouted. He glanced quickly at the tiring-room doors, thinking he might have been heard. When no one came out, he turned back to Ben.

"I feel wretched about it," he said miserably. "Though I didn't know Tom the Teeth was doing the stealing. But when I heard Garth's name, it near froze my blood. For though I never set eyes on him before – and did not know it was he who pushed past us in the tiring room – I know he's as bad as they come!"

But Ben was growing excited, for he had seen a way forward. He remembered the promise he had made to himself, to help the company any way he could. Now, here was a chance.

"Well, then – do you have any idea where someone like Samuel Garth might be found?" he asked.

"What if I did?" Matt asked, frowning. "You're not thinking of looking for him yourself, are you?"

"I'm offering you a bargain," Ben answered. "You help me find Garth, and I keep your secret."

Matt stared at him. "You're mad," he said.

Ben returned his gaze. "Well, if I am, are there not places where only a madman would go?" he asked. Then an idea burst into his mind. "Or a villain!" he added. "If you know of places where a man on the run might hide, where no one would ask questions…" He broke into a smile. "It wouldn't be too difficult for either of us, would it? We could play a pair of thieves. Then if we catch sight of Garth, we—"

"Do you know what you're asking?" Matt broke in, aghast. "Have you any idea what could happen to us in such places, if someone realizes what we're doing?"

Ben gave a shrug. "I can guess. But I'm going to search anyway. So – are you going to help me, or not?"

Matt opened his mouth, then closed it. He knew that once Ben got an idea, there was no point in trying to talk him out of it. He looked away, and gazed into the fire again.

"Well…I suppose there's one place we could try," he said.

Dusk was falling when the two boys made their way down to the Falcon Stairs and hailed a boat. That was Matt's idea: it was a long walk across London Bridge and through the city to its west side and beyond. They might find the gates shut by the time they got there. But by boat, it was a very short way: almost directly across the river.

They were going to Whitefriars, an old monastery that had long ago fallen into ruins. It was outside the city wall, and had once been a place of sanctuary, where criminals could avoid arrest. Those rights had been abolished in the time of King Henry VIII, though debtors might still claim refuge. But it remained a known hideout for people on the run from the law. In the dark corners of Whitefriars, they felt safe.

Though he was excited, Ben felt uneasy, and somewhat ashamed of himself. He knew John would be worried about him, but he hoped it would not be for long. He had told Will Sanders that he was off on an errand, and would make his way home later. Before Will could protest, he had hurried away. What Will did not know was that while Ben was talking to him, Matt was helping himself to a few things from the costume store. Once away from the Rose, the two had changed out of the cherry-red doublets which made them so conspicuous, into old clothes which were too big for them. After roughing up their appearances, Ben hoped they would pass for a couple of cutpurses. Matt had found an old, blunted dagger, a stage prop, which he had fixed to his belt. Beyond that, they would have to trust to the dim light – and to luck.

After a while a boat arrived, and the two climbed aboard. Then they were out on the water, with a cold wind blowing. Ahead of them, lights showed from the city. But when they told the waterman where they wanted to go, the fellow looked puzzled.

"Whitefriars?" he echoed, as he heaved on his oars. "Why there?" When neither boy answered, a frown came over the man's features. "In trouble, are you?" He shook his head, and gave a sigh. "So young, too... What on earth is the world coming to?"

Nevertheless, he changed his course and took them across to a rickety set of stairs that creaked when the sculler bumped against them. While Matt clambered ashore, Ben found two halfpennies and paid the fare. As he stepped onto the jetty, the man pointed vaguely. "Your way is through there," he said. "It isn't far – but have a care where you walk!"

Ben nodded, and pulled down the cap he was wearing. Without a word, he followed Matt, who was disappearing into the gloom.

Whitefriars was a frightening place, full of shadows. Ben knew it was a ruin, but he had not expected it to be such a warren. He and Matt walked between tumbledown walls and deserted courtyards, past passages leading away into darkness. Here and there, crude shelters had been built – and from the glow of small fires within, it was clear they were inhabited. But Ben's spirits sank as he looked about. Now that he was here, he felt far less sure of himself than he had been back at the Rose. How would he begin his search in a place like this?

"Well, I've brought you here," Matt said.

The two boys kept close together. Even Matt was nervous, Ben could tell. Trying to master his own fear, Ben said: "Let's get started, then. We know what Garth looks like—"

"Keep your voice down!" Matt hissed. "It's not wise to draw attention to yourself." He felt for the stage dagger at his belt, and seemed reassured by it. Taking a breath, he turned to Ben.

"Listen," he said, "if anyone asks, your name's William, mine's Henry. We picked pockets in East Cheap market, and nearly got caught. That's why we're here…" He glanced about. "We'll go up to each fire, ask if we can warm ourselves for a bit. Then we'll move off, after we've got a good look at whoever's there. Understand?"

Ben gave a nod.

"But if we're lucky enough – or unlucky enough – to set eyes on Garth," Matt went on, "one thing you mustn't do is let him know you've recognized him. And I only hope he doesn't remember either of us from the Rose – or we're finished!"

"All right...Henry." Ben gestured to the nearest fire, and summoned all his courage. "Let's get warm, shall we?"

So the young players began their hunt among the ruins for Samuel Garth – the man who had tried to kill Hugh Cotton. And it was that thought, more than anything else, that made Ben stick to his plan instead of getting away from this fearful place, as he would have preferred to do.

Darkness had fallen now, but there was a little moonlight. The pair of them went to one fire after another, asking if they could warm their hands. To Ben's surprise, they were usually allowed to draw close. Sitting or standing about the fires in small groups were men and women of all ages. Some were ragged folk, others looked so ordinary that Ben wondered what made them seek refuge here. No one, to his relief, asked him or Matt any questions, and their false names were not needed. Once or twice they found themselves backing away, when it was clear they were not welcome. For there were bad men here too – Ben saw it in the dark looks he and Matt got when they walked up. But at least no one threatened them. It was cold now, and both boys were glad of whatever heat they could get. They were hungry too, and the smell of food being cooked over some of the fires made them want to linger. But each time, after they had managed to scan the faces, Matt nudged Ben in the ribs to signal that they should move off. And nowhere, to his growing disappointment, was there any sign of the man he remembered running through the tiring room after he had stabbed Hugh at the end of *The Witch of Wandsworth*.

After nearly an hour of wandering about Whitefriars, Matt was ready to give up. Even Ben had to admit that it looked like a wasted journey. They had been to every fire, and seen no one they recognized. Finally they stood by the river, just above the jetty. They had been round in a circle, only to end up where they started.

Matt was glad it was over. "Well, you've only one way to get home, Buttonhead," he said, beating his arms to his sides against the chill. "For it's past curfew, and the city gates will be shut by now. You'll have to walk up to Ludgate Hill, then all the way round the outside of the walls, and cut through Moorfields to Bishopsgate Street."

Ben made no reply. Not only was he cold and hungry, he was bitterly disappointed. And he was angry with himself, too. He had deceived John and Will, and gone off on a fool's quest. More, he had forced Matt to be his accomplice. He gazed unhappily across the river, where the watermen called to each other in the dark. The small lanterns hanging from the sterns of their boats bobbed about like fireflies.

"I'm sorry," he said. "I shouldn't have made you come."

After a moment, Matt shrugged. "It was worth a try, I suppose," he muttered. "Though in truth I'm glad we didn't find him. For if he'd recognized us..." He broke off with a shiver.

As if it were catching, Ben shivered too. "Can you get home?" he asked.

Matt nodded. "It's low tide now." He pointed to where a strip of shingle, a few feet wide, showed along the water's edge. "I can walk down the river, then climb the stairs at Queenhithe, and go through to Thames Street. Our house isn't far."

Ben was about to take his farewell when there

came a splash of oars, barely yards away. A boat was coming up fast out of the dark. And by some instinct, both boys stepped back from the jetty, darted behind a broken-down wall and crouched out of sight. Neither of them spoke, but Ben knew that they had done right. Perhaps it was because the boat's lantern was not lit.

There was a crunch of gravel: the sculler had run aground on the shore beside the jetty. And now there were voices: two men – no, three. As Matt and Ben peered from their hiding place, they saw figures moving about in the boat. Then one climbed over the side, cursing as he landed heavily on the ground. The other put a hand out to steady himself, whereupon there came a third voice. This was clearly the waterman, who now struck a flame and lit his lantern. Then he held it up – whereupon Ben gave a start. For the two passengers were visible in the lantern's gleam. The one who had jumped from the boat turned – and Matt and Ben stiffened from head to foot.

It was the man they had been searching for: Samuel Garth.

There was no mistaking him – Ben felt his neck-hairs stand up. A cold fear stole over him, as he remembered the stubby fellow pushing him and Matt aside as he ran through the tiring room that day, a scowl on his sweaty face...

Matt's hand gripped his arm, so tightly that it hurt. Leaning close, he spoke hoarsely in Ben's ear.

"The other one... Do you see who it is?"

The man who had stayed in the boat was of a different stamp from his companion. He was heavily built, wearing a cloak and a tall hat. Beneath it, a thin face showed, with a nose like a hatchet...and it was all Ben could do not to cry out.

Alderman Gilbert!

Chapter Thirteen

For a minute, Ben and Matt stared in amazement. Then they saw that Alderman Gilbert was not getting out of the boat as Samuel Garth had done. Instead, he lifted his hand and threw something over the side to Garth, who caught it. Even from a distance, the chink of coins could be heard.

"That's the last of it! And think yourself lucky. For if you come back to Bankside, I'll have your tongue cut out! That'll stop your careless talk!"

Gilbert spoke in the angry tone Ben remembered from when he had first seen the man on the morning after the fire. The words chilled him as he watched, crouching in the dark. Beside him, he sensed that Matt was as tense as he was.

And now, Samuel Garth spoke. "This is Whitefriars Stairs," he said in a harsh, throaty voice. "You said you'd take me to Ivy House..."

"Are you mad?" Gilbert was scowling at the man in the lantern's gleam. "I can't be seen there – and nor should you! Walk upriver to the watergate, and ask for His Lordship's steward. Wait until he comes out. He'll pay you what remains – then you can get yourself to Dover, take ship for France. Or anywhere, for that matter – so long as you're gone!"

Garth muttered some reply, but it looked as if the men's business was over. The waterman, who had been growing restless, blew out his lantern and quickly stowed it away. Then he put his oar over the side and pushed hard. The sculler lurched, then slid off the shingle into deeper water. Without a word, Alderman Gilbert turned his back and sat down. The waterman plied his oars, and in a short time the boat had disappeared.

Samuel Garth watched it fade into the darkness, then turned to face upriver. For a moment he stood sniffing the air like an animal, his squat figure etched against the moonlight. He weighed the purse in his hand, so that the coins jingled again. Then he set off along the strand, his boots crunching on the gravel. Soon he too had vanished in the gloom.

Ben turned to Matt – only to read the warning in his eyes.

"If you're thinking of following him," Matt said, "then don't! He'll be armed, and on the alert. He'd stick us both as soon as he'd stick a rabbit for his supper!"

Ben's mouth was dry. The sight of the man he had been searching for scared him, yet he was tingling with excitement. A few minutes ago, only a long, gloomy walk home had stretched ahead of him. Now, everything had changed.

"You've done your part," he said, "and I'll keep your secret, as I promised. But I can't let Garth get away!"

"Use your head," Matt retorted. "You heard where he's going – Ivy House. It's one of the mansions that line the river all the way to Westminster. Whoever this lord is, it sounds like he's paying Garth for his services, as Gilbert did." He paused, frowning. "If you ask me, from what Gilbert said, Garth went to him for more money. Looks like he's been hiding out here after all…" He let out a breath. "Now I think myself lucky, for I'm glad we didn't stumble across the fellow!"

But Ben shook his head impatiently. "Don't you want to know who it is who's paying him?" he asked. "The one they called His Lordship?"

"They're all *His Lordships* in those great houses," Matt told him. "There's Essex House, where the Earl of Essex lives, then Arundel House, then Somerset House – I think Ivy House is the next one. It won't be hard to find out who lives there."

"But by then it could be too late," Ben argued. "He'll have taken ship, as Gilbert told him to…"

"It's a long way to Dover," Matt replied. "And if I guess right, he'll be on foot." He grimaced. "Believe this, Button: I want to see the man caught as much as you do. He was no friend to my father – he's hard and cruel, and looks after none but himself!" Then Matt fell silent. And seeing the sense of his words, Ben sighed.

"All right," he said. "I'll go home and tell John. He'll know what to do."

"What will you say," Matt asked him, "when he asks why we went to Whitefriars?"

Ben stood up stiffly. "I'll tell him it was my idea," he said. "Just a notion I had…"

It was more than an hour later before Ben finally arrived at Hog Lane, footsore and weary, and walked into the Symes's house. It had been a long, cold journey around the outside of the city walls, but it had passed without mishap. And as he had expected, once he was home he found himself in trouble. John and Alice Symes were angry, but he knew it was because they had been worried about him. Ben answered their questions truthfully, leaving out only the part about Matt knowing who Samuel Garth was. But when he spoke of what had happened at Whitefriars Stairs, John was astounded.

"Gilbert...?" He shook his head. "It can't be... Are you certain it was him?"

Ben nodded, and recounted the conversation between the alderman and Samuel Garth, as well as he could remember it.

John and Alice glanced at each other. They were in the kitchen, where Ben could warm himself by the fire. Alice was heating up some milk for him. The thought of hot porridge and bread cheered him a lot.

"Ivy House..." John was frowning. "But that's where Lord Brooke lives." When Ben looked blank, he added: "He's the Earl of Horsham!"

Ben's eyes widened. "Then Horsham's Men are behind everything that's happened to us, after all!"

John did not answer. Alice had taken the hot milk from the fire and was pouring it into a bowl.

"You'd best sit," she said to Ben, who wasted no time in taking his stool at the table. While Alice mixed the porridge with a wooden spoon, she spoke to John.

"So this business at the Rose goes deeper than you thought."

John looked bewildered. "I don't understand," he said. "I know James Mostyn... He's not above a few sly tricks against a rival company, but I still can't believe he would have anything to do with the other things: the fire, or sawing through a gallery post – let alone the attack on Hugh."

Ben's thoughts were whirring about again. But John saw how tired he was, and his expression softened.

"I was angry with you for going off like that," he said. "Though I see you were trying to help. But that was a foolish thing you did, wandering about Whitefriars."

"It was indeed!" Alice startled Ben by plonking the bowl of porridge before him. "And another thing – what's become of your new doublet?"

"Matt and I hid them – they're safe," Ben replied. The smell of hot porridge was in his nostrils, and he grabbed his spoon and began to eat. He was so hungry that he forgot about everything else until he had wiped up every last trace of the porridge with a hunk of rye bread. Only when he had finished did he notice that John had gone out, and Alice was sitting opposite him, working at her embroidery frame.

She looked up, and seeing the question already on his lips said: "It can wait until morning. You should go to bed now."

Ben gave a huge yawn. As usual, Alice was right.

The next day, Friday, John Symes called Lord Bonner's company together at the Rose. And to their surprise, Hugh Cotton arrived to join the gathering. He looked tired and pale, and walked stiffly, but it was clear that he was recovering from his wound. It cheered Ben to see him, as it did everyone else. Even Will grinned when Solomon made jokes about Hugh getting himself stabbed as an excuse for not doing any work. For a moment, the players seemed to have forgotten their troubles. They gathered round the brazier in the yard, all talking at once – for the news was encouraging. A carpenter had been to look round the theatre, and found that no other timbers had been tampered with. He had repaired the damaged one. So now, at least according to Gabriel Tucker, there was no reason why they should not reopen –

apart from Alderman Gilbert, of course, and his order signed by the Privy Council.

But when John told the players what Ben and Matt had learned the previous night at Whitefriars, there was amazement all round.

"I knew it!" Gabriel quivered with indignation. "It was Horsham's Men all along... They're in league with that dry stick of an alderman to drive us out of Bankside! He had a hold over Tom the Teeth and forced him to steal from us – then he hired Garth to do the real dirty work, and paid him off!"

He threw an approving look at Ben and Matt, who were standing together. "And if it hadn't been for our plucky prentices, we'd never have known it! I think they deserve our thanks!"

Ben glanced at Matt, who kept his eyes lowered. The two of them had not spoken about the night before except to John, and to Will Sanders when they returned the costumes they had taken. But Will seemed to have so much on his mind, he had merely grunted at them.

Now John raised a hand. "Gabriel is right," he said. "But we need to think hard about our situation. I went to Constable Micklewright first thing this morning and told him everything – yet he still wants proof before he will act. But I have better news: last night I received word from Lord Bonner. He'll be in London by tomorrow – and he's our best hope of justice." He frowned. "For if the Earl of Horsham himself is involved, as it now seems, I'm unsure what to do."

The others were eager to speak – but at that moment their attention was diverted by footsteps. Everyone turned to see two familiar figures walking in through the doorway. One was Simon Jewell; the other was the playmaker, Daniel Rix.

John Symes was surprised, but gestured both men forward. There were greetings – but Simon Jewell looked grave. He nodded to the rest of the company, who made room for the newcomers by the fire, then addressed John.

"I heard the gossip, from a couple of players," he said. "I didn't know what to make of it…" He shook his head unhappily. "Tom the Teeth's vanished without a word – and I thought I was his friend." He turned to Daniel Rix, who was looking out of place as usual. He still wore his old mouse-grey suit, and his fingers were stained black with ink.

"Then today I ran into your playmaker," Jewell went on, "who's as anxious as I am. Is that not so, Master Rix?"

Rix cleared his throat and summoned a smile.

"Indeed…the fact is…well, I'm getting rather worried about *The Witch of Wandsworth*," he stammered. "I mean, with things as they are, you know…but in any case…" He looked at John. "Master Jewell and I would like to share your troubles, Master Symes – I mean, help if we can. That is, if you'll let us." He coughed nervously. "What say you? Will you at least tell us what's happening?"

After a moment John smiled. And Ben's heart lifted as he saw the relieved looks on the faces of all the players. Suddenly, it seemed as if Lord Bonner's Men were not so alone after all.

A half-hour later, the company were sitting in a close group around what had become their regular table in the back room of the Elephant Inn. They had talked, then eaten and drunk, then talked again. And now at last the whole story of the cruel plot against Lord Bonner's Men was plain to see. For, as Gabriel had said, the Earl of Horsham seemed to be behind the sabotage directed against the company. And from what Ben and Matt had overheard, Alderman Gilbert was carrying out his wishes. The worst part of it was that he had hired the wicked Samuel Garth, who would stoop even to murder. Now that they turned the matter over for what seemed to Ben like the tenth time, it was enough to make the bravest of men quail.

John looked round the table. "I won't go to the constable again," he said. "Instead I'll report Samuel Garth to the mayor and the city fathers. They can send horsemen along the Dover road to overtake him – assuming he's on his way, which seems likely. As for Gilbert…" He spread his hands helplessly. "It's hard to see how we can prove his involvement."

He glanced at Ben and Matt. "Like it or not," he went on, "it's the word of two boy players against that of an alderman of this ward – an important man." He sighed. "And you know how players are regarded – as little better than rogues!"

"Rogues perhaps – but not villains!"

There was an intake of breath from everyone, and all eyes went to the door. Whereupon their surprise was quickly tinged with anger. For standing in the doorway was the last person anyone expected to see.

James Mostyn, leading player with the Earl of Horsham's Men.

Chapter Fourteen

"*I* bear no flag of truce, masters, as you did that time at the Swan..." Mostyn stepped warily into the room. "Yet I hope the tavern counts as neutral ground?"

Nobody spoke. Gabriel Tucker bristled and Will Sanders glowered, but they kept their seats. The others merely stared.

"Well...you've a nerve, I'll say that." John Symes eyed the man, and Ben was reminded of the two players' meeting, a week ago by the Falcon Stairs. But this time, Mostyn's manner was different. He appeared nervous, as well as worried.

Mostyn hesitated, then seemed to gather his courage. "There have been rumours flying about Bankside," he said, "ever since the attack on Master Cotton..." He glanced at Hugh. "I hope you will believe me when I say I'm glad to see him recovering."

At that there were exclamations, and Gabriel Tucker sprang to his feet. "How dare you!" he cried. "Things have become a deal clearer since we came to your theatre, fellow! In fact, what we've learned might put you in jail, and the rest of your rabble along with you!"

Mostyn was about to reply, but John stood up. And the look on his face was enough to make Gabriel sit down again.

"You'll forgive us if we don't make you welcome, James Mostyn," John said quietly. "But Gabriel speaks true: we know that your own patron is involved in the mishaps that have befallen us since we came to Bankside." He paused. "I suppose you'll deny it—"

"Will I?" Mostyn's voice was sharp. Several of the company, Ben included, had begun to wonder why this man had taken the risk to come here. Now he seemed not only worried: he was angry too.

"There are rumours," Mostyn repeated, "and gossip is rife. But when was the theatre world free from that?" He drew a breath. "Well – suppose I wish to hear what you have discovered? Would you care to tell me?"

This was unexpected. But after a moment, John nodded. There and then he gave a quick account of all that had happened in the past few days. And as the players watched James Mostyn, they grew puzzled – for the man was thunderstruck. He sank down upon a stool, and by the end of John's tale he was gazing at the floor. Finally he looked up.

"I suspected something," he said in a shaky voice. "But not this..." He sighed. "I'm at a loss to know what to do."

Lord Bonner's Men exchanged glances. "What did you suspect?" John asked sharply. "Tell us!"

Mostyn hesitated. "At least, with Tom Towne's confession, you know now that none of my company stole from you," he said. "And that we had no part in the fire, or the attack on Master Cotton. As for sawing through a gallery post..." He frowned. "That was a desperate act – no player would do such a thing!"

"Yet it seems Samuel Garth would," John countered. "What of him?"

"I never heard that name until now," Mostyn answered firmly.

"And Alderman Gilbert?" Simon Jewell spoke up. "Will you deny that you know him, too?"

"Gilbert?" Mostyn shrugged. "He's no friend of ours either – he's a killjoy who dislikes all players."

"Yet he has not closed your theatre down!" Gabriel cried.

"No, he has not," Mostyn agreed. "Nor has he troubled us since you came to Bankside." He frowned again. "If I swore to you that I knew nothing of this campaign to ruin Bonner's Men, would you believe me?" he asked.

There was some muttering. But Ben had been watching Mostyn, and felt certain that the man's surprise was genuine. He seemed truly dismayed by what had happened.

"Why should I believe you?" John asked. "Especially after what your prentices did to our boys..."

Mostyn looked ashamed. "I knew nothing of that until some days later," he said. "I'm truly sorry for it..." He turned to Ben and Matt. "I know what Edward Ratcliff is like. Yet he's a good player..." He sighed. "The other boys – Gadd and Laney – he rules them. They always do what he says."

He paused. "But in any case, from what I've learned, Master Button and Master Fields gave as good as they got." He glanced at John. "They're a plucky pair, your prentices."

John gave a nod, but was eager to return to the matter in hand. "Yet you talk in riddles," he said. "How can you claim you know nothing of the campaign against us, when there's open rivalry between our companies? Everyone knows it!"

"Fair competition is one thing," Mostyn answered, "but sabotage and attempted murder are quite another." He drew a deep breath. "You're luckier than you know, masters," he said to all the players, "in having a kindly patron who values you, and treats you well. We are not so fortunate."

Then the man stood up. "I thank you for honouring our truce," he said. "Now that I know what hurts you have suffered, I wouldn't blame you if you'd seized me..." He met John's eye. "I can only repeat that I was not a party to these crimes against you. Nor can I give you any answers. I fear you must look elsewhere for those."

Mostyn moved towards the door, then stopped and turned. "And if I guess aright, you may not be out of danger, even now!"

He pulled the door open and went out, and Lord

Bonner's Men were too surprised to follow him. They merely stared at the door as it banged shut, then at each other.

That afternoon, the company rehearsed some new songs, with more enthusiasm than they had shown in days. Simon Jewell played a lute, while Solomon had his drum about his neck. As usual, Ben and Matt sang the treble parts. All of them were glad to forget for a time that the Rose was still closed to the play-going crowds, while the Christmas Revels drew ever nearer. But the prospect of Lord Bonner's arrival the next day gave them hope. After leaving the Elephant, John Symes had gone to report Samuel Garth to the authorities. And to the players' surprise, when John returned he looked more cheerful than he had done all week. So of course Solomon Tree had to make a joke about it.

"If you've found a purse outside, then I think we should all have a share of what's in it," he muttered.

John gave him a wry look. "No purse, master comedian, but some news," he replied. "For the hunt is on for Samuel Garth. It seems he's known as a dangerous fellow, who's been in prison. An order's gone out for his arrest."

Ben and Matt exchanged looks, while the players gathered round on the stage, encouraged by the news. But it was Simon Jewell who asked the difficult question.

"What about the Rose reopening, Master Symes?" he enquired. "Did you raise that subject?"

John shook his head. "They wouldn't listen to me. Alderman Gilbert seems to have a lot of influence..." He sighed. "If I could hurry matters forward, I would do so," he went on. "Yet when all's said and done, I'm still a common player. That's what one of them called me. And soon after that, they showed me the door!"

"What sort of door was it?" Solomon asked, with his deadpan look.

A smile tugged at John's mouth. "I can't say I took any notice," he answered.

"There you have it," Solomon said gloomily. "If you'd told them what a fine door it was, they might have been more polite. And more helpful too."

There were some sniggers. Then, seeing Solomon's glum face, someone laughed aloud.

Solomon turned mournfully to him. "That wasn't a joke," he said. "Just an observation."

But now someone else gave a chuckle. Suddenly, snorts and giggles were breaking out on all sides. Ben found one welling up inside him, too. He looked at Matt, and saw that he was grinning. Then, as if the whole company had somehow been given permission, a wave of laughter broke over them. Soon everyone was howling, as if they had just heard the best joke of the year.

It was a curious sight. Gabriel was hanging on to Will, who was bent double, guffawing into his beard. Hugh had to sit down on a bench, as if laughing was painful for him – as well it might have been. Simon Jewell and John Symes merely stood and laughed until tears came to their eyes, while Ben and Matt were now laughing so much, they slumped down on the stage. Only Daniel Rix stood in silence, dumbfounded by what was happening. And finally, everyone noticed him.

"Sorry..." The playmaker spread his hands. "I...I confess I don't see cause for such merriment..."

But that set them laughing all over again. It was as if, after a week of disasters, the company had suddenly recovered their sense of humour. Sometimes, Ben remembered, laughter was the best medicine. He lay on his back and let the laughs pour from him. Beside him, Matt started rolling around, which only made everyone laugh harder. It struck Ben that anyone passing by the theatre might think there was a performance on after all.

But it was then that a clear voice rang out from the yard below them, and in a second everyone fell silent.

"So – this is how you spend your time!" Lord Bonner shouted. "I've a good mind to dismiss the whole lot of you!"

John Symes was the first to recover. He hurried to the edge of the stage and made a hasty bow. Behind him the others turned in confusion, and those with hats quickly removed them. Ben and Matt scrambled to their feet. Every eye was upon the company's patron, whom they had not seen in months.

"Your pardon, My Lord." John looked embarrassed. "We did not expect you until tomorrow…"

"So I see!" Lord Bonner retorted. He was wearing a new black velvet doublet and a crimson cloak, while the peacock feather in his hat wobbled in the air. A fine gold chain lay upon his chest. Behind him stood two servants in the same red livery that the players wore.

"Well now…" The patron glanced at the rest of the company, who quickly made their bows. "I arrived early and thought to surprise you, but I had no inkling I would find the doors shut, and my players engaged in such tomfoolery! What does it all mean?"

John cleared his throat. "It's a long story, My Lord," he answered. "Did you not receive my messages?"

"Messages?" Lord Bonner snapped. "I've been travelling for the past fortnight. What were they about?"

John swallowed. "Then, you don't know about our invitation to play before the Queen at Whitehall?"

Lord Bonner snorted. "Of course I know about *that*! It was arranged long ago…" He frowned. "Do you mean to tell me you're not ready for the Christmas Revels? They begin next week!"

"I know, My Lord…" John looked round helplessly at the company. "The new play will be a great success, I'm sure…" Seeing Daniel Rix standing with a forced smile, he pointed. "Here's our playmaker… Master Rix?"

At his gesture, Rix shuffled forward and bowed so low his beard brushed his shoes. Straightening up, he murmured: "It's titled *The Witch of Wandsworth*, My Lord… My finest work, you see…that is, well, I think it is…"

"Indeed?" Lord Bonner glared at the playmaker, who winced, then turned back to John. "Master Symes," he said in a calmer voice, "I'm getting a stiff neck looking up at you like this. Kindly come down here and explain matters to me. On second thoughts," he added, "all of you come down!"

So, looking uncomfortable, the players filed out

through the tiring room and made their way down to the theatre yard. As Ben came out he heard Matt whisper: "Now we're in for it!"

The company stood before Lord Bonner like school children about to be punished. But before John could make his explanations, His Lordship fixed them all with his fierce stare, and said: "Whoever closed the Rose down had no right! My players must be allowed to rehearse for the Queen's Revels. You there, what's your name...? Rix!" He pointed at the playmaker, who blinked.

"Have you made up playbills for the new piece?" he demanded. "If so, why aren't they on every post and every tree trunk between here and the Bridge?"

Rix looked dismayed, but Will Sanders spoke up quickly. "It's my task to get the bills printed, My Lord," he said. "I put some up last weekend, but since we got closed down I haven't thought upon it..."

"Then kindly think upon it, and put them out!" His Lordship snapped. He turned to John. "Now, who was it who ordered the theatre closed?" he asked.

"Alderman Gilbert, My Lord," John answered. "After we had a...well, a bit of trouble, he came in with a paper signed by the Privy Council..."

"Did he, now?" Lord Bonner glared at him. "Then you'd best leave him to me." His gaze wandered over the rest of the company. Ben gulped as it came to rest upon him.

"Master Button." His Lordship favoured him with a nod. "I'm glad to see you again..." He glanced at Matt, standing beside Ben. "Who are you?" he barked.

Matt bowed and gave his name, at which His Lordship merely grunted. Then at last he turned back to John.

"Come with me now, and tell this long story of yours," he said. "As for the rest of you, you'd better get to work. For make no mistake, the Rose will reopen tomorrow!"

Then, as everyone gaped, their patron strode off towards the doors, with John hurrying after him.

Chapter Fifteen

The next day was Saturday, and despite the theatre being about to reopen, Ben was allowed to be late for rehearsal. Once again it was time for his fencing lesson at Carlo Bonetti's, which he would not miss for anything. What was different today was that Matt Fields was allowed to go too, for his first lesson. Matt had been told of this at the end of the previous afternoon, to his great delight. John had informed Lord Bonner of everything that had happened in the last week or so. And the lesson was His Lordship's reward to Matt for standing up to Horsham's boys with Ben, thereby saving the honour of Lord Bonner's company. Matt lost no time in reminding Ben of it, when they met outside the fencing school.

"His Lordship's paying for my lessons out of his own purse," he said.

"He pays for mine, too," Ben told him.

"But it's results that count, isn't it, Buttonhead?" Matt retorted. "I'm a quick learner. I'll soon be featuring in fight scenes, while you're still standing there screaming and looking scared."

Stung, Ben turned upon him. But just then the door of the school opened as someone came out. From inside, a familiar voice called, "Signor Ben! Why you stand there? Come in from the cold!"

Carlo was in good humour this morning. As the two boys entered, he was already taking a foil from the wall. But when he saw Matt, his eyes widened.

"Another one? Maybe I start new school, for boy actors only!"

Matt blinked, but Carlo laughed and threw him the small sword. With some difficulty, Matt caught it by the handle.

"Good!" Carlo nodded approvingly. "We make rapier-and-dagger man of you too. What your name?"

Whereupon Ben saw his chance. "This is Fly-spot," he said at once. "He may not look much, but he's a quick learner."

Matt rounded on him angrily, but he was too late.

"Welcome, Signor Fly-spot!" Carlo said. "First I show you how to stand and crouch. You watch me – I'm friend to Rocco, who was greatest fencer in London. He used to make his pupils wear lead weights if they not nimble. You ready?"

Matt swallowed, then gave a nod. Meanwhile Ben smiled broadly, and went to choose a sword for himself.

It was a busy morning. But Ben had to admit that Matt could indeed be a quick learner when he chose. He mastered the fencer's crouch, and by the end of the lesson he was trying his thrust and parry. But when he asked Carlo to show him the *imbroccata*, the master shook his head.

"You not ready, Signor Fly-spot. Next time, maybe."

"My name's Fields," Matt said. "Matthew Fields…"

But Carlo had turned away to shout at a young man who was not doing his exercises correctly. So he did not see the door open, or the people who came in. But Ben did – and tensed from head to foot.

"Well now – what a surprise. It's the Cherry-tops."

Edward Ratcliff entered the room with a swagger, his eyes fixed unwaveringly upon Ben. Behind him came Tom Gadd, his long hair tucked into a cap, and the spindly figure of Richard Laney. All three Horsham's boys halted, staring at their enemies. And at the sound of Rat's voice, Matt Fields swung round, to gaze with Ben at the newcomers.

The silence was broken by a clash of rapiers, followed by Carlo shouting at the man who had earned his displeasure.

"No, signor butcher! You not cutting lamb chop, you fighting for your honour – even your life! Now try again, like proper fencer!"

Rat waited for the men to resume their practice, then spoke again. "You knew there'd be a reckoning, Button," he said softly. "And today's as good a day as any."

Ben said nothing. By instinct he and Matt moved closer together, as they had done when they last faced these three, in the snow on Bankside. Rat's glance strayed to the swords hanging on the walls and, without a word, he and his companions moved towards them. But before any of them could take one down, Carlo's voice rang out.

"You! Leave that foil alone!"

Rat turned, a scowl on his face. "I was going to have a practice," he began.

But Carlo was angry. He strode across the floor, his own sword in hand, and stood looking down at Rat. The two other boys took a step back, but Rat stayed where he was.

"I tell you last time, Signor." Carlo wagged his finger at Rat. "I no want trouble here, like you do before..." He glanced at Gadd and Laney, who flinched.

"So you bring your friends, too," Carlo went on. "Well – if they want lessons they can stay, but not you! You not welcome in my school. Carlo will not teach a boy who won't listen to him, or do his proper moves!"

Ben and Matt glanced at each other. But when Ben looked at Rat again, the boy was pointing directly at him.

"I challenge this one to a bout!" he said, and turned to Carlo, whose mouth fell open. "A fair contest, with tuck or foil," Rat went on. "You can be umpire, Master Bonetti, and see fair play. My friends will stay back – as my opponent's friend must. Now, what say you?" And before the astonished Carlo could answer, he added: "Or are you afraid to let your pupil show how poor a fencer he is?"

There was a silence. The other people in the big room had stopped their exercises, and Ben found that all eyes were on him. He drew a deep breath, and said: "I accept the challenge."

Carlo gave a start. "You not ready, Signor Ben," he said, frowning. "This boy has come here more times than you—"

"You heard him – he accepts," Rat interrupted. "Or was it only because he knew you wouldn't allow it?" He turned to Ben with a cruel smile. "Perhaps he's a coward after all," he sneered.

Matt took a step forward. "We know who the cowards are," he said. "Those who come with billets out of the dark, three against two who were unarmed, and set on them—"

"Enough!" Carlo threw Matt a look which silenced him. Turning to Rat again, he raised his sword and pointed.

"This is fencing school – not bear pit!" he cried. "I teach a noble art, for gentlemen. Is not for boys with grudges, to fight like in school! Signor Ben learn so he can fence onstage, at *teatro*. I teach him to use sword to defend himself. But you!" Carlo's dark eyes blazed, so that sparks seemed to fly from them. "You bully, Signor. So – *sputo*! Carlo spits on bullies! Now get you gone!"

Another silence followed, and it was a very uncomfortable one. Rat glowered – at Carlo, at Ben and Matt, indeed at the whole room. But it was clear that he was not going to get his way. With an angry swipe of his hand, he turned on his heel and made for the entrance. Gadd and Laney hesitated, then followed. But at the door, Rat turned and, ignoring Carlo and everyone else, pointed at Ben.

"You're lucky once again, Button," he said. "But mistake me not: I'll have revenge. And you'll be sorry you made me wait!"

Then he was gone, and his companions with him. As the door closed, Ben looked round to see Carlo gazing intently at him.

"I not like it, Signor Ben," he said in a quieter voice. "I see there's bad blood between you and this boy…so now you make Carlo a promise, eh?" When Ben nodded, he went on: "You swear to me you never fight with real swords, over grudge. Or else one of you get hurt – even killed! You understand?"

"Yes, Master Carlo," Ben answered. "I promise I'll do as you say."

Carlo nodded, and began to relax. "Same for you, Signor Fly-spot," he said, turning to Matt. "You promise too?"

"I do, master," Matt said. "But I'd be glad if you

called me by my real name. It's Fields..."

But Carlo was already looking away, shouting at his older pupils. "What you wait for, Signor?" he bellowed. "Crouch and show me your *stoccada* – quick!"

With a sigh, Matt turned to Ben.

But Ben had not heard the exchange of words between Matt and Carlo. He was staring at the door, through which Rat had disappeared a moment ago.

He knew that the feud between himself and Master Ratcliff wasn't over.

Half an hour later, Ben and Matt made their way through the crowds that thronged London Bridge. The sun had come out, and a fresh breeze was blowing downriver. Ben had managed to put his encounter with Rat out of his mind. But he was thoughtful as the two of them emerged on the Southwark side of the river – where they both stopped abruptly. For on the wall of the Bridge gatehouse a new playbill had been pasted, where anyone who passed would see it.

THE WITCH OF WANDSWORTH, it announced, in letters several inches high. *By D. Rix, gentleman. To be played today and until Christmas at the Rose by the Lord Bonner's Men, as it was played on Monday last to great acclaim, and will be played before the Queen. God save Her Majesty!*

Matt broke into a smile. "He's done it!" he exclaimed. "His Lordship has thwarted old Gilbert and got the Rose reopened, as he promised he would. We've got a performance after all!"

Ben found himself grinning, too. "He always keeps his promises," he said. "So it's the witch's costume for me again, and Lady Celia's for you – even if it's not the lilac gown."

Matt grunted. "I don't mind what I play, or what I wear," he answered. Then he brightened again. "Do you think they'll let me join in the sword fight?"

Ben blinked. "You've only had one lesson!"

"But I was watching everyone," Matt argued. "It's not so difficult, whatever Master Carlo says..." He frowned. "Which reminds me – next time, you can tell him my real name!"

Ben put his hand to his ear. "Sorry, I didn't hear that," he said.

They had turned into Horseshoe Lane. Ahead, the Rose towered over the rooftops. And on every wall and every gatepost, indeed wherever they looked, there seemed to be another playbill announcing *The Witch of Wandsworth*.

"Will must have been busy," Matt remarked.

Ben was thinking of his witch's role, and hoping he could remember all his lines. There were quite a lot of them. They rounded the end of the horseshoe, nearing the theatre. There was no one about yet, for it was barely midday, and performances did not start before two of the clock. Ben was about to speak to Matt when there was a sudden noise, behind and to his left, from an alleyway between houses. He looked round – then in an instant everything went dark, as a thick, foul-smelling cover was pulled roughly over his head.

"*Mmmm! Ggnnn!*" Ben struggled wildly, his voice muffled. He grabbed at the thick material and realized it was a sack – it smelled of hops, which brewers used to make beer. But strong arms took hold of him and pinned him tightly as another pair of hands drew the sack downwards, almost to his knees. Desperately he kicked out, and got only a sharp blow to his ribs in return. Now his hands were being bound... He gasped, fighting for breath, as the sack was tightened about him. Close by, he heard Matt grunting and struggling, and knew that both of them had been seized. He began to fight harder, but it was no use. Then fear gripped him, for he began to feel faint...he might suffocate! Try as he might, he realized that he could not escape, for the arms that held him were far stronger than his. And the next moment, he was lifted off the ground and swung through the air, to land with a thump across what he guessed was someone's shoulder. Then, like a sack of coal, he was being carried away, bumping against the back of whoever was holding him.

It was stifling in the sack. Sweat broke out all over Ben's body. He took a big breath, intending to shout as loudly as he could – but the sack was dusty, and the dust went straight to the back of his throat. Then he was coughing and spluttering, his chest tight... He wriggled, and tried to kick again, but whoever was carrying him simply tightened their grip, so that the last of the air was driven from his lungs. In his mind's eye, lights floated about...

And then it really did go dark.

Chapter Sixteen

*I*t seemed like hours, but it was only minutes later when, like coming up from the bottom of a deep pool, all at once Ben was conscious again. He realized that he must have blacked out. He had no idea where he was, for everything was in darkness. He was lying on a cold stone floor, with his head against a wall and the smell of hops still in his nostrils. But thankfully the sack had been taken off him, so at least he could breathe properly. His hands were not tied any more, either. Then he heard a sharp movement nearby, and sat up with a start.

"Ben?" It was Matt. "Are you all right?"

"Yes," Ben answered, much relieved. "Are you?"

"I think so…" Matt's voice came eerily out of the dark. He shuffled forward across the floor, until he was close to Ben. "I'm not sure where we are," he said, "but I think it's a cellar. I can smell wine."

Ben smelled it too. "You're right," he said. "Who was it, do you think? Who grabbed us, I mean."

"I don't know," Matt replied. "But I've an idea *why* they did it."

"You have?" Ben asked – then at once he too guessed why. And it made him angry, as well as fearful.

"The campaign against us," he said. "It isn't over, is it?"

"No." Matt sighed. "Since all of London must know by now that the Rose has reopened, someone's up to their tricks again. Now they've gone in for kidnapping!" He gave a short laugh. "Makes you feel important, doesn't it?"

"Important?" Ben echoed. "What do you mean?"

"I mean that one sure way to stop Lord Bonner's Men from playing would be to whisk both their prentices away, wouldn't it? Even with someone standing in for Hugh, there isn't time to rehearse another boy in your part – or mine. Not for the Christmas Revels, anyway."

It was true: the boy players were vital to the company. Without Ben in the witch's role, and Matt in Lady Celia's, *The Witch of Wandsworth* couldn't be performed. Ben was dismayed. While part of him was flattered to think how valuable he was, another part of him was worried – not so much for himself, as for Lord Bonner's Men. Things would go badly for them if they could not perform. At the least, they would be discredited, and made to look foolish.

"You have to admit it's a clever plan." Matt's voice came out of the blackness again. "For who would believe John, or any of the others, if they said both their prentices had vanished into thin air? People would just think we'd run away. Bonner's Men would be a laughing stock among the theatre folk – and some other company would be eager to step forward and play for the Queen instead of us!"

"Like Horsham's," Ben said thoughtfully.

"Yes!" Matt almost shouted. "It's been them all along. No matter what Mostyn said yesterday in the tavern. They've been trying to ruin us ever since we came to Bankside!"

Ben was thinking hard, for in his mind a lot of things were falling into place. "Not merely to ruin us," he said quietly. "It looks to me now as if what they wanted all along was to stop us playing at the Christmas Revels."

Matt was silent for a while, but Ben knew that he too was thinking over all that had happened. It seemed so obvious now that Ben wondered why he had not guessed sooner.

"And Alderman Gilbert," he said. "He's a part of it... After what we saw and heard at Whitefriars..."

"I haven't forgotten," Matt retorted, somewhat crossly.

"Are your hands tied?" Ben asked, after a moment.

"No – are yours?"

"No," Ben answered. "So let's take a look around, shall we? See if we can find a way out of here."

But Matt's reply was disheartening. "Don't you think they'll have thought of that?" he asked bitterly. "We're in a cellar, without windows. All we'll find is a door, and you can bet your life it's locked."

"Well, anything's better than just sitting here," Ben told him. He reached out and felt the wall behind him. The stonework was cold to his touch, and damp too. He got on his knees and moved his hand along the wall, then stopped when he bumped against something solid.

"Here's a barrel," he said. "This is a wine cellar all right."

"Clever thinking." Matt's voice was harsh in the darkness. "And there'll be no way out!"

Ben ignored him. After a while he got to his feet, and began feeling his way around the room. He found more barrels, of various sizes, from hogsheads as tall as he was, to small kegs. Some were full or half full, others empty. Then he gave a start as he trod on something. There was a yelp, and he knew he had stepped on Matt's hand.

"Watch where you're going, Buttonhead!" Matt cried.

"Sorry," Ben muttered. "Look, why don't I move along to the right, and you go left?"

"So which way is left?" Matt asked in a sarcastic voice.

"I don't know..." Despite the plight they were in, Ben found himself growing impatient with Matt, as usual. "At least we can find the door, can't we?" he demanded. "Then if anyone comes in, we'll know which way to face."

"What makes you think anyone will come?" Matt asked.

Ben hesitated. "Surely someone will, sooner or later—" he said, but Matt interrupted.

"How do you know? If no one knows where we are, they could just leave us here to starve. Have you thought of that?"

"That's looking on the gloomy side, isn't it?" Ben countered, frowning to himself. "You and Solomon should get together..." He trailed off, as an uncomfortable thought struck him. Those who had plotted against the company, like Samuel Garth at least, had been bold enough to stoop to setting fires – even attempted murder. Why should they stop now?

"You see, Button?" Matt's tone was close to despair. "You've worked it out too. We're stuck here until someone rescues us – or comes in by accident. But by then, all they might find are our dead bodies!"

Ben drew a deep breath. "Well, pardon me if I don't give up just yet," he said. "If you don't want to help, stay where you are, and I'll work my way around you."

But at that there came a sound, and with some relief Ben realized that Matt too was getting to his feet.

"You go that way," he said, "I don't want you stepping on me again." And his hand came out of nowhere, to shove Ben aside.

"All right!" Ben retorted. "And if you come to a door, tell me."

But it was Ben himself who found the door, just a minute later. He had felt his way around a stack of small kegs covered in cobwebs. Then he found a door frame, and then the door, which seemed very solid. Groping downwards, he felt the bottom of the door, and found there was a step below it, down to the floor. Feeling upwards again, he found a handle, and with growing excitement pressed it. He felt the latch rise, and pushed, but nothing happened. He pulled the door towards him, and still nothing happened. So he rattled it, gently at first, then harder. Then in sheer frustration, he banged upon it. But there was no sound from anywhere.

"What did I tell you?" Matt's voice floated towards him across the room. "We're prisoners, Button... under lock and key, as sure as if we were clapped up in the Clink!"

Ben heard him slump to the floor. "Now I know how my father felt," Matt said unhappily. "For I've ended up in jail – just like him!"

Hours passed. Ben had no idea how many, but he thought it must be night by now. Sitting on the cold floor, back against the wall where he had first found himself, he struggled not to give in to despair. The company would have had their performance – that is, if they had been able to: most likely they would have cancelled it, which meant they would lose more money. He thought of John: his master would be very worried about him, as would all of Lord Bonner's Men. But surely, he reasoned, they knew he and Matt would never go off like this? Perhaps they were searching for them already – the thought gave him hope. Wherever this cellar was, he guessed it was not far from Horseshoe Lane, where they were captured. Likely they were still on Bankside – it would have been difficult for their captors to transport them across the river in broad daylight. So surely someone would hear them, sooner or later?

But he had tried shouting for help already, soon after he found the locked door. Even Matt had joined in, having mastered his feelings. Both of them had called out together, as loudly as they could – but there was no answer. They might have been at the bottom of a well for all the good it did.

Ben shuddered, and realized that he had fallen asleep. He did not know for how long, which was worrying. He sat up and tried to rub some life into his cold limbs. He was hungry now, and very thirsty. He turned towards where he had last heard Matt's voice, and called, "Are you awake?"

Matt too must have been asleep. He stirred, and Ben sensed that he was sitting up.

"I am now," Matt grumbled. "How long has it been, do you think?"

"I don't know…" Ben sighed and sat back against the wall. The thought struck him that if they got really thirsty they could always try to break open a barrel of wine. Though he knew that would not ease his thirst for long – in the end it would only make it worse. Moreover it would make him drunk, and that would not help him at all.

"Wait…listen!" Matt whispered – and Ben tensed, for he heard it too: a sound, beyond the door. The next moment he was scrambling to his knees, and heard Matt do the same. There was the squeal of an old lock, followed by the scrape of the door upon flagstones. Both boys were blinded by the light that flooded into the room. The door stood wide, and, on the step above them, a figure was visible behind the beam of a lantern. Then Ben and Matt jerked in alarm as someone spoke.

"Supper time, my little moles!" There followed a laugh that was almost a cackle, and it shook Ben. For a moment he thought it was the Witch of Wandsworth, come leaping out of his dreams.

But there was no mistaking it: their jailer, if that was the right word for her, was an old woman. Setting the lantern down by the door, she waddled down the step into the cellar. She wore heavy skirts, and was carrying something. The two boys blinked, struggling to adjust to the light. And at last Ben saw the face: it was thin and heavily lined, with a pair of watery eyes that peered at them. Wisps of grey hair poked from under the old woman's cap, which was dirty and frayed at the edges.

"I'll set it here," she croaked, and bending stiffly, put something down on the floor. It was a dish, which was followed by a tin jug. Then she straightened up, wheezing, and surveyed her prisoners.

"You haven't touched any wine, have ye?" she screeched. "For master would be mighty displeased by that! Anyway 'twill do ye little good, for 'tis strong drink, for strong men!"

She gave another cackle, as witchlike as the first. "Now make yourselves comfy, for you'll likely be our guests for a few days yet." The woman coughed horribly, then spat in the corner, before getting her breath back.

"Don't fret – you'll not be harmed," she said, "as long as you don't try any tricks! For I've a stout truncheon here, would crack your heads open!" She cackled again, and patted her pocket. "Be good moles," she went on, "and in a while you'll be freed. Though 'tis not my place to decide when..." She sniffed, then stepped back and caught up the lantern by its handle.

"Eat well, my beauties..." The woman turned, lurched up the step and through the doorway, and pulled the door shut. Darkness returned in an instant. The noise of the lock jarred in Ben's ears, as if it had screamed at him. Then there was a brief footfall outside, followed by silence.

In the dark Ben heard Matt give a sigh of helplessness which was close to a sob.

But he did not blame him at all. For now, he felt close to tears himself.

Chapter Seventeen

*A*fter they had eaten, both boys were so tired that they slept for some hours. When Ben woke up he guessed it was morning, even though the room was still in darkness. He stretched himself, then got up and groped his way to the door. Feeling around it, he found the keyhole, bent down and put his eye to it – and was rewarded by a tiny glimmer of grey light. He straightened up, and tried to rally his hopes. Outside it was daytime – in fact, as far as he could judge, it was Sunday.

He was about to make his way back to his place by

the wall, when there came a faint sound that stopped him dead. In a moment he was on his knees, pressing his ear to the door – and at once he knew he was not mistaken: from somewhere nearby came the ringing of church bells. What was more, he recognized the peal – it was St Saviour's church! He had been right in thinking they were still close to where they had been captured. Which meant they were close to the Rose, too.

Ben felt his way back to the far wall, and bumped into Matt's sleeping form. Matt woke with a cry, and sat up.

"What are you doing?" he demanded.

Ben told him about the glimmer of light, and the bells. But Matt merely sighed, and sank to the floor again.

"What use is that?" he asked. "We may as well be right next to the Rose, for all the good it does us. We're stuck here until that old crone – or her master, whoever he is – lets us out!"

Ben sat down, hugging his knees. It was cold in the cellar, and he shivered. He reached out and found the water jug, from which he and Matt had drunk thirstily the night before. It was empty – he remembered now that they had drained it, as he remembered the stale bread and the pieces of dry beef that had made up their supper. But both of them were so hungry, they had eaten every scrap.

After a while, Ben got to his feet again. The worst thing about being a prisoner, he decided, apart from the dark, was having nothing to do. He took a few paces across the room and back – he was beginning to know it as well as he knew his attic room back home at the Symes's house in Hog Lane. The memory of it came to him with a rush that made him sad. Already it seemed an age since he was there.

"This is no good," he said, and tried to shake himself out of his gloom. "We've got to make some sort of plan!"

Matt snorted. "Like what? Tunnel our way out, like moles – isn't that what the old witch called us?"

Ben tried to think clearly. But his spirits were sinking, for he knew as well as Matt did that there was no escape from this place. Restlessly he moved to the door, but misjudged its position and bumped into one of the barrels.

Then it came to him, with such clarity that he sat down with a thump.

"What's happened?" Matt called. "Are you hurt?"

Ben's mind was whirling. "The kegs," he said – and suddenly he wanted to laugh. "They're our weapons – they're all around us!"

"What are you rambling about, Button?" Matt asked sourly. "You mean to try and knock the old woman out – before she can reach for her truncheon? Assuming she comes back, that is."

"Not quite," Ben said. He groped about and found one of the small kegs, which was covered with dust. He tilted it onto its side, then rolled it across the floor towards Matt. Matt gave a start as the keg bumped into him.

"What's this?" he muttered. "What scheme are you cooking up now?"

Ben told him. And by the time he had finished, his fellow prisoner was listening intently.

"Well," he said at last. "It's not much, but it's worth a try."

In the dark, Ben grinned for the first time since he had been brought here. There was still hope, after all.

It was the longest day Ben had ever known. He and Matt had worked out what they would do, but that was hours ago. To pass the time, they talked. Matt spoke of his family, and the good times he had had in London before his father began drinking heavily. Ben's father, too, was dead, but that had been of a sickness. Unlike Matt, he was from a country village.

The woods and fields had been his playground when he was small, not the streets and markets Matt knew. Perhaps that was why the two of them were so different, he thought.

They guessed that it was evening – the time when the old woman had brought their food the day before. And now, both boys grew tense. They knew they had but one chance to carry out Ben's plan; they would not get another. And at last, just as Ben felt he couldn't bear to wait much longer, there came a footstep outside, and the squeal of the key again. But by then, both of them were in their places. Everything was ready.

As before, when the door opened, the light was dazzling. The old woman lifted her lantern, and saw what looked like two sleeping forms against the wall. She took a step forward, and the familiar, raucous voice called out: "What's this, young moles – asleep? I've brought you a treat this time – a chicken leg each!" She gave her cackle. "Now that's better than a poke in the eye, ain't it?"

There was neither sound nor movement from the huddled shapes. So, muttering to herself, the old woman set her lantern down and descended the step, which was her undoing. For, as her foot came down, the floor seemed to roll away from her. With a shriek she flung up her arms – but it was too late. She lost her balance, and when she took a clumsy step sideways the floor rolled from under her other foot! She had stepped on the keg Ben had slid beneath her – and suddenly there were several of them, rolling all around her. With another cry, she landed on her back, and the platter she was carrying crashed to the floor, sending chicken legs flying. And only now did the old woman realize that her prisoners were not by the wall at all – but on either side of the doorway, behind her. With a howl, she tried to right herself, like a huge beetle struggling on its back. But she knew she had lost – whereas Ben could have shouted for joy. His plan had worked!

There was no time to waste. Leaving their doublets and jerkins where they had placed them, wrapped round small barrels, Ben and Matt leaped up the step and stumbled through the open doorway. Behind them, their jailer howled again – this time more in rage than in pain. Then her cries faded, as the pair hurried along a passage. To their relief, there was a dim light ahead.

They skidded to a halt: the light came from above – there was a staircase before them. Behind them, the old woman was screeching, and it was only a matter of time before someone heard her. So gathering their courage, they began to climb the stairs. After a few steps, there was a left-hand turn. Matt, who was ahead, peered round the corner, then froze.

"This is a big house!" he whispered over his shoulder. "How will we find our way out?"

Ben crouched beside him and looked for himself. Both boys were wearing only their shirts, hose and shoes. But they were too excited to feel cold – and in any case, warm air was now drifting towards them. Peeping up the stairs, Ben saw a hallway, with a chest against the wall and tapestries hanging above it. At the end was a window, but no door.

"We'll have to chance it," Matt whispered. "I'm not going back in that cellar – I'd rather die!"

Ben saw the determined look on his face. Meeting Matt's eye, he nodded: he too would risk anything rather than remain a prisoner. "I'm with you," he said.

Whereupon Matt turned and crept up the last few stairs, with Ben close behind. Luckily there was no one about, so they moved softly along the hallway... Then they turned a corner, and stopped.

The hall broadened out, with doors on either side – but straight ahead of them was a wider one, which must lead outside. The two of them exchanged glances – they dared not wait. And now, from below, the old woman's cries could be heard again... Bracing themselves, they ran forward – when, to their dismay, a door opened on their left. It was between them and the way out!

Ben's heart thudded. His breath tight in his throat, he flattened himself against the wall. Matt did the same beside him. Wide-eyed, the two stared at the open doorway – but to their surprise, all that came out was a cloud of steam. Then a manservant appeared, carrying a huge platter heaped with roasted fowls. The man's face was red and shiny with sweat – for of course, he had come from the kitchens. As both boys held their breath, the door across the hallway also opened – and at once a babble of voices flooded out. The household were sitting down to supper!

The servingman was looking straight ahead. Clouded in steam, he walked with measured steps across the hallway towards the parlour where the diners were. He did not see Ben or Matt. Then he was gone, and the door banged shut behind him.

The boys could hardly believe their luck. They glanced at each other, then tiptoed forward past one closed door, and then another. The front door was near now, the voices loud from the room at their right. But in a moment they had passed the door and, quickening their pace, they approached their goal: the way to freedom. Ben's heart was in his mouth as he saw Matt reach out... Escape was close! And luck must be with them, for the cellar below them was now silent.

Matt's hand closed upon the door handle, an iron ring carved in the shape of a wreath. He turned it, and the door opened. He threw a look of such triumph back that Ben could have laughed. In a second they would be out. Dim light appeared through the gap, and a cold breeze blew in – outside, darkness was falling. Matt stepped back and pulled the heavy door wide – whereupon disaster struck.

From the hallway behind them came a great howl, and both boys snapped round – to see their jailer hobbling round the corner, a bony finger pointing at them, her crabbed face twisted in fury. And Ben's heart dropped like a stone.

"Stop them!" the crone yelled. "The moles are loose! Stop them, for mercy's sake!"

The door was open, and Matt leaped through it like a deer. Ben followed, scraping his shoulder on the frame in his haste. Behind him, there were shouts. He risked a look round, and saw a man hurry into the hallway. The man stopped, his gaze swinging between Ben and the old woman, who was standing motionless, still screeching.

Then the man too shouted – in a voice that would have stopped an avalanche. "Arrest the fugitives! Seize them!"

Ben was out of the door – but his shock was so great that he faltered. For staring at him, with a face like thunder, was the man he had last seen in a boat being rowed away from Whitefriars Stairs.

It was Alderman Gilbert – and this was his house!

Gilbert shouted again, people appeared from the room behind him, and at last Ben recovered his wits. With a leap, he was down some steps, landing heavily on the ground. He saw lights in the distance. Before him was a garden with a wooden gate. Even as he raced towards it, he saw Matt Fields vault over it. Matt paused and looked back.

"Come on!" he cried. "Keep up!"

Ben ran to the gate, gripped its top rail and threw himself over. His heel brushed the woodwork, but he landed on both feet. Then he was running, not heeding the footfalls or the shouts that spilled from the house behind him.

There were trees... He saw Matt ahead, dodging around them as he ran. But to his dismay, he did not recognize this place. If he knew where the river was, or from which direction the bells of St Saviour's had come, he could get his bearings... Breathing hard, weak from hunger and thirst, he slowed to a trot, looking to right and left... Then he realized he had lost sight of Matt.

But the shouts from behind were louder, so he began to run again...through the trees, where it was becoming too dark to see. Then there was another shout – and this time Ben halted.

It had come from ahead. And now he saw a figure blocking his path – and froze. For there was no mistaking the face that materialized out of the gloom.

Rat Ratcliff. And it was hard to say who looked more surprised – he or Ben.

But somehow, Ben found new strength. In a second, he had swerved aside and was running through trees again, into darkness.

Chapter Eighteen

After a short time the trees thinned out – and again there were lights ahead. By instinct, Ben veered away from them. He did not look back – but he heard the thud of running feet, and knew that Rat was close behind. Then, as he passed the last tree and emerged into the open, Ben slowed down. There were more lights in the distance, somehow reflected on the ground in front of him. Then all at once, he knew where he was. The reflection came off water – he was in the Pike Garden! And sure enough, when he looked to his right, the towering bulk of the Rose was dimly visible through the gloom. So Alderman Gilbert's house was south of Horseshoe Lane... Ben had been running north-west, at an angle towards the river. At last, he had his bearings.

Then he risked a look behind, and tensed: out of the trees, Rat came running.

He was short of breath, yet he wore the same scornful expression that Ben remembered from Carlo Bonetti's. But at least the boy was alone, without his two henchmen. Swiftly Ben glanced around. There was no one to help him. He must face his enemy by himself.

"You've led me a merry dance, Cherry-top!" Rat drew to a halt a few yards away, panting. There was a cruel light in his eye, as he contemplated revenge upon the boy who had thwarted him in the snow by the riverbank, and again at Carlo Bonetti's. Ben did not answer, but stood his ground and waited.

But Rat was in no hurry. He took a few steps, until there was but a couple of yards between them, then stopped and made a sudden, backward movement. Ben gave a start: the boy had whipped a poniard from his belt. The blade gleamed in the half-light as he held it out before him.

"We've no foils, so I can't out-fence ye, Button!" Rat's voice was cold as steel. "So I'll content myself with sticking you, like a hog at slaughter!"

Still Ben said nothing, which seemed to anger his adversary. "Lost your voice, have you?" he sneered. "Or scared speechless?"

Ben met the other's eye. Suddenly, he felt quite calm. He had known there would be a reckoning between Rat and himself – and now, here it was. In a way, it was a relief. The worst that could happen was that he got stabbed. Even that, he thought, was better than going back to the cold cellar at Alderman Gilbert's. At least he had shaken off pursuit from that direction.

"What were you doing, skulking about round here?" Ben asked. And then a thought leaped into his mind with such force he almost gasped.

"Looking to set another fire at the Rose, were you?" he added.

Rat gave a start – and Ben knew he was right! It all made sense now. Samuel Garth had been hired to kill Hugh, but the fire in the storehouse had been started by someone closer to hand – Rat Ratcliff!

"So...Alderman Gilbert paid you too," Ben said. "To warn us off, by burning the store-hut down—"

"Stop your mouth!" Rat cried. He darted forward and made a swipe with his poniard. But Ben was quicker – he jumped back and avoided the dagger's blade.

"And now the Rose is back open," Ben went on, "you're trying it again. Well maybe this time you'll go to jail for it!"

"But it's your word against mine, Button," Rat breathed. "And you won't be alive to point the finger!" With that he lunged, forcing Ben to dodge aside. But the blade caught him on the arm – he felt a jab of pain, and winced. Luckily the cut was not deep. He was on his feet still...

"Is that your best stroke?" he said, though he was panting now. "You're out of condition. No wonder Carlo wouldn't teach you—"

But he broke off then, as Rat gave a snarl of rage and leaped forward once more. And this time, Ben lost his balance. There was a root or dead branch in the grass behind him, and his foot caught on it. He toppled over backwards – and in a moment Rat was upon him, knees astride his body. Ben saw the wicked gleam in his eye...and the next few seconds seemed to last for minutes.

With crystal clarity, Ben saw Rat raise his poniard. He reached up and grabbed him by the wrist, but knew he was not strong enough. Desperately he struggled to ward off his assailant – but now it was only a matter of time. Thoughts raced through his brain: where was Matt? What were those lights he had seen? And worst of all: was he about to die?

There was a shout, then another. They came from Ben's right... He snapped his head round, and saw lights again – then his heart sank. They were torches, coming closer, and they were held by running figures: Alderman Gilbert had caught up with him. He was finished.

With his strength ebbing away, Ben strained against Rat's arm, and for a moment the poniard was poised in mid-air, its deadly point quivering as each boy fought for mastery. But as Ben weakened, the blade began to descend. He braced himself, waiting for the pain...

But it never came.

There were more shouts, giving way to cries of alarm. Lights danced before his eyes and feet pounded towards him, so that the very ground shook. Rat span round, and gave a cry. Faces appeared, even as he sprang to his feet – but he was too late. Strong arms seized him. The poniard flashed in the torchlight, and was wrenched from his grasp. Then he was crying out in rage as his arms were pulled roughly behind him. And as Ben looked up, open-mouthed, someone bent over him.

"Thank the heavens!" John Symes, torch in hand, sank to his knees beside him. "I've searched every inch of Bankside since yesterday." There were tears in John's eyes. He put out a hand to grip Ben's shoulder. "The others too," he went on, recovering his breath. "They swore they wouldn't rest until we found you...even if we had to tear down every house!" He shook his head. Then he saw the blood on Ben's shirtsleeve, and started.

"You're hurt!"

Slowly, Ben sat up. Relief flooded over him like a warm shower of rain, making him quite giddy. He propped himself on his elbow, and tried to smile.

"Sorry I missed the performance," he said. Then his face clouded. "Have you seen Matt? He was ahead of me..."

There were others now, crowding round Ben, torches held aloft. He looked up and saw Lord Bonner's Men, their faces taut with concern: Solomon, and Gabriel with his twitching moustache, and Will, and Simon Jewell... Then he sighed with relief. For pushing through them was a shorter figure, who now peered down at him.

"What's the matter, Buttonhead," Matt asked. "Couldn't you keep up?"

Then, slowly, he grinned. And all Ben could do was return his grin, and sink back gratefully onto the ground.

Chapter Nineteen

Three days later, which was a Wednesday, the sky may have been slate-grey and the air chilly, but there was a warmth inside the Rose Theatre that would have melted a block of ice. Ben felt the excitement as he and John Symes walked through the doors to find the company already busy. Today, however, there was no rehearsal. Lord Bonner's Men had packed their prize possessions – their costumes and props – in baskets and chests, ready for carrying to the riverside. It was the day after Christmas, and a boat would soon arrive to transport them up the Thames to Whitehall Palace.

So much had happened, since Ben had been rescued at the last moment from the clutches of Rat Ratcliff. After he and Matt had been given warm clothes, a message went straight to Lord Bonner at his town house near the Tower of London. Then, finally, Constable Micklewright had arrived and, after hearing the players' tale, had marched Rat off to the Clink prison. In the end, Rat had not been so brave as he made himself out to be: he had fallen to his knees, crying for mercy. Ben and Matt had stood together, and watched him taken away.

The cut on Ben's arm was not too serious, and Will soon bandaged it. Then the whole company had gone back to the Rose to give Ben and Matt food and drink, and hear their story. But when it emerged that they had been held captive in Alderman Gilbert's house, there was outrage.

"He planned all along to wreck our chances of playing before the Queen." John faced the company, and there was anger in his eyes. "He it was who hired Samuel Garth – and Rat too, without even Mostyn knowing of it. Gilbert got us closed down just as he wanted – just as he forced Tom the Teeth to steal from us by buying up his gambling debts."

He shook his head, and fell silent. The others were quiet too, as they thought of the wickedness that had been heaped upon them. But it was not until later, when Lord Bonner himself arrived in a hurry, that the whole truth was known. And that was a revelation.

Fixing them all with a grim look, His Lordship made his announcement: "I've just come from the Privy Council. They have ordered the arrest of the Earl of Horsham!"

And while his company listened, standing around the brazier in the theatre yard, Lord Bonner spoke of the plot that had been hatched against him and his players.

"I had to be certain before I acted," their patron told them. "But as soon as I was, I went to the Council. Alderman Gilbert is already under arrest. I have also learned that a man named Samuel Garth, though disguised, has been caught on the Dover road. And he will be hanged at Tyburn!"

Loud conversation broke out, as everyone took in the news. But Ben and Matt glanced at each other, and were silent. They could not forget Whitefriars, or the sinister look of the fellow as he sniffed the air.

And now, Gabriel Tucker could not help speaking up. "So I was right, My Lord!" the little man cried. "Horsham's Men were out to ruin us all along – I said so, from the very beginning!"

There were some frowns, but Lord Bonner was not

angry. "Not his men, Master Tucker," he said. "But the Earl himself, his hireling Ratcliff, and Alderman Gilbert." He turned to the others. "But none of you could know what lay behind it," he went on. "For the treachery was not really aimed at you, my friends: it was aimed at me!"

Then His Lordship told them of the corrupt Earl of Horsham, and his thirst for power; and every one of them listened in silence, as the night wore on and the fire burned low.

"You know I'm a good friend to our Queen," he said, not without a note of pride. "And, of course, some are jealous of me... Men like Edmund Brooke, the Earl of Horsham. But that is not what drove him to such desperate lengths to stop you from playing at the Christmas Revels: it was his hopes of becoming Lord Chamberlain."

His Lordship paused, looking round at his players. "It's likely you do not know that Lord Hunsdon, the Lord Chamberlain, is gravely ill," he went on. "He may not live long. So already some noblemen are hoping to secure his important post for themselves. Among them is Horsham. He knows I'm one of those who might be made the new Chamberlain..." His Lordship allowed himself a little smile. "And he hates me for it!" he went on. "If his players had been allowed to perform at Whitehall instead of mine, he would've had the chance he needed to speak to our Queen and present her with gifts, to gain her favour. His difficulty was that my company had been invited already. So if he could wreck your chances, he could offer his own players in your place. And as we know now, he was prepared to use any means, including sabotage and murder, to ruin us! When even those failed to stop you –" His Lordship smiled at them – "for you're a stubborn lot, when you choose to be – as a last resort, he had Gilbert arrange the kidnap of our prentices, meaning to keep them hidden away until the Revels were over!"

At last, His Lordship had turned to Ben and Matt. And to their surprise and embarrassment, he had shaken each of them by the hand.

"Gilbert has a poor opinion of theatre folk," he said. "And he reckoned without our two plucky boy players, who were able to make their escape. Though I for one would not have doubted you."

He smiled at the two of them. "My thanks to you both," he said. "You have earned my gratitude – and no doubt the Queen's too, when I tell her of it."

Ben and Matt were so stunned by that, they could think of nothing to say. And soon afterwards they had been taken home to recover from their ordeal:

Matt to his mother in Thames Street, Ben to Hog Lane, where Alice scolded him as she fed him and cleaned the cut on his arm, then sent him to bed.

But tired as he was, Ben could not sleep. So he was still awake a half-hour later, when footsteps sounded on the ladder, and John's head poked above the opening.

John had sat on a stool by the bed, and told Ben news that cheered them both. For it seemed that James Mostyn had come to him, to ask pardon for what his patron had done. Though now that it was known that Horsham's players had not really been to blame, John was ready to put rivalries aside, and the two men had shaken hands. Mostyn, he said, was saddened and filled with remorse for the things his prentice, Rat, had done.

"At least now," John said, "his other two boys, Gadd and Laney, are free of the older one's wicked influence. The company will seek a new patron, and try to make a fresh start." He sighed, and Ben was glad to see the weight lifted from his shoulders. Clearly it had cheered John to make peace with his old enemy.

Later, as Ben drifted into sleep in his attic chamber, he found himself thinking of the storehouse fire again. He stirred as flames rushed towards him.

Then they turned into a lantern, and once again he heard the old woman's cackling voice. He awoke with a start, only to realize that he had been dreaming of his witch's role. So he turned over, and slept soundlessly.

Ben and Lord Bonner's Men played *The Witch of Wandsworth* at Whitehall Palace before the Queen and her glittering court, with great success. So many people came to see them that the palace chambers seemed to be at bursting point. Again and again they were asked to perform the piece, so that their fame spread beyond Whitehall, to the company's delight. For they knew that they could perform the play anywhere after this – on Bankside, or back in Shoreditch. And even Master Shakespeare's company would not be able to stop the crowds from flocking to see them.

Also delighted was Daniel Rix, playmaker, who was at the palace to see his work performed. And when he was allowed to kneel before the Queen, and present her with a book of poems he had written, he was a very happy man indeed.

"*The Witch* is my best work, you see," he said later, when he took supper with the company. "Always knew it...though I confess the jokes are... well, not the finest ever written..." He turned to Solomon Tree. "I have to admit that Constable Clout was better, after you, er..."

"Spiced him up?" Solomon said, glum-faced as ever. "Well, someone had to." Then he brightened. "But I had a thought the other day: how about you and I doing a book of jokes together? You could present that to the Queen, too..."

But at that Master Rix choked on his food, and everyone had to thump him on the back until he recovered.

And there were other things to cheer Ben that Christmas. He had played the witch well, and been applauded warmly for it – as Matt had too, in his role as Lady Celia. But they would not always be prentices, Ben knew. He looked forward to being skilled enough – and tall enough – to sword fight onstage. It just seemed to take such a long time, growing up.

The best performance at the palace, the company all agreed, was the last: the one when Hugh Cotton returned, now well enough recovered to play the hero Adam Ardent, and show off his swordplay. Though, once again, Ben and Matt were not allowed to take part in the fight, but had to watch through the back curtains. Only when it was over, and the hero had triumphed to cheers and applause, did the two boys turn to each other.

"I could have done that," Matt said. "I told John, but he wouldn't listen."

"A good thing he didn't," Ben muttered. "One fencing lesson, and you think you're a swordsman. Everyone onstage would've been in danger with you flailing about."

Matt flushed. "Who asked for your opinion, Buttonhead?" he retorted. "Next time we're at Carlo's, we'll have a bout and see who comes off best!"

Ben was about to make a retort of his own – then a thought struck him. And instead of getting angry, he smiled.

"Talking of Carlo," he said, "do you think you'll ever get him to stop calling you Signor Fly-spot?"

Matt drew a sharp breath, and would have grabbed hold of Ben. But just then the curtain was yanked aside, and Will Sanders's face appeared.

"You two – onstage, now!" he hissed. "It's time to take your bows – what kept you?"

Matt let his arm drop. Then, without a word, the two of them walked out into the light of a hundred candles.

*

That night, after the company had taken a late supper, Ben wandered, tired but happy, through the torchlit passages of Whitehall Palace. Soon he found himself at a set of doors that he knew led to the riverside. There were two burly guards there with halberds, but one of them recognized Ben, and they did not challenge him. So he was allowed to walk out onto the Privy Stairs, the big covered jetty which the Queen used when she took to the river in her royal barge.

It was a clear, frosty night, but Ben did not mind the cold. He gazed out at the great River Thames, glittering under the starlight, and wondered whether Jack Pike was out on the water somewhere. He looked forward to climbing into the old man's boat once again, and hearing his stories.

In fact there were quite a lot of things to look forward to, he thought sleepily, as he gazed up at the vast canopy of stars overhead. Downriver, to his left, the lights of London glowed. On the far side, he could see a faint gleam from Bankside. He thought of the Rose Theatre, and all that had happened since Lord Bonner's Men had moved south of the river. It had turned into an adventure, all right – but not one he could have imagined. He shuddered, thinking of the dangers he and the others had faced. But then, it had come right in the end... In fact, Ben realized, if he had the choice all over again, he would have gone there in any case. After all, the company triumphed: Lord Bonner's Men were becoming the most famous players in London. And Ben Button, featured boy actor, had now performed before the Queen herself. It brought a glow of pride that warmed his heart. And what further adventures might yet lie ahead of him? he wondered.

He took a last look at the rippling surface of the river. The twelve days of Christmas were over, and soon the company would be back in the Old Theatre at Shoreditch. Ben would be able to take Brutus out for walks again, every day if he wished.

Turning away, he walked back indoors. He passed the tall guards with their halberds, and was surprised when one of them smiled at him.

Then he realized that he was smiling himself.

Usborne Quicklinks

For links to websites where you can see the remains of the Rose Theatre, take a virtual tour of Shakespeare's Globe and explore London in Elizabethan times, go to the Usborne Quicklinks Website at www.usborne-quicklinks.com and enter the keyword "traitor".

Internet safety
When using the Internet, make sure you follow these safety guidelines:

- Ask an adult's permission before using the Internet.
- Never give out personal information, such as your name, address or telephone number.
- If a website asks you to type in your name or email address, check with an adult first.
- If you receive an email from someone you don't know, don't reply to it.

Usborne Publishing is not responsible and does not accept liability for the availability or content of any website other than its own, or for any exposure to harmful, offensive, or inaccurate material which may appear on the Web. Usborne Publishing will have no liability for any damage or loss caused by viruses that may be downloaded as a result of browsing the sites it recommends. We recommend that children are supervised while on the Internet.

Don't miss Ben Button's first adventure...

ELIZABETHAN MYSTERIES

Rogues' Gold

Ben is excited about his first summer tour with Lord Bonner's Men, as he's never travelled beyond the city of London before. But their first stop at Bowford Manor turns to disaster, when one of the group is accused of stealing a valuable gold plate.

Ben teams up with Lady Sarah, and they discover that dangerous secrets surround the mysterious plate. And some people will stop at nothing to prevent the truth being discovered...

ISBN 9780746078792

Out now!

About the author

John Pilkington worked in a research laboratory, on a farm, and as a rock guitarist in several bands before realizing he wanted to write. After taking a degree in Drama and English, and acting and directing for a touring theatre company, he began his professional writing career with radio plays. He has since written plays for the theatre and television scripts for the BBC. He is also the author of a series of historical crime novels, and a non-fiction book, *A Survival Guide for Writers*. *Elizabethan Mysteries* is his first series for younger readers.

Born in Lancashire, John now lives in Devon with his partner and son.